## Praise for Fatal Forgery

"I loved the sense of place, with some surprising
revelations about jail and courthouse conditions and
operations, and an interesting change of setting at one
point, which I won't reveal for fear of spoiling the plot.
There was great attention to detail woven skilfully into
the writing, so I felt I learned a lot about the era by
osmosis, rather than having it thrust upon me. All in all,
a remarkable debut novel."
*Debbie Young, author and book blogger, UK Ambassador for
the Alliance of Independent Authors*

"From the start of this story I felt as if I had been
transported back in time to Regency London. Walking
in Sam's footsteps, I could hear the same cacophony of
sound, shared the same sense of disbelief at Fauntleroy's
modus operandi, and hung onto Constable Plank's coat
tails as he entered the squalid house of correction at
Coldbath Fields. I am reassured that this is not the last
we shall see of Samuel Plank. His steadfastness is so
congenial that to spend time in his company in future
books is a treat worth savouring."
*Jo at Jaffareadstoo, Amazon "Top 500 Reviewer"*

# FATAL
# FORGERY

Susan Grossey

CreateSpace Independent
Publishing Platform

This novel is a work of fiction. The events and characters in it, while based on real historical events and characters, are the work of the author's imagination.

Book layout ©2013 BookDesignTemplates.com

Fatal Forgery/ Susan Grossey -- 1st edition
ISBN 978-1489587404

*For Paul,*
*who rarely complained when I spent so much time with*
*the other man in my life – Constable Samuel Plank*

*Trust not too much to appearances.*

—VIRGIL

# CHAPTER ONE

# Cannot this business be settled?

## FRIDAY 10TH SEPTEMBER 1824

On the day of the arrest, it was Daniel waiting to deliver my messages. He stood on my doorstep, dancing eagerly from foot to foot – six or seven, I reckoned he was, although he himself couldn't tell me, and filthy as they come. No son of mine would have been allowed to get into that state, not with my Martha's fondness for soap and water, but back then we were still waiting and hoping. I tore the page out of my notepad and folded it into four, the writing hidden on the inside – force of habit, as Daniel couldn't read a word. I reached into my tunic pocket for a coin and the lad's eyes followed my hand hungrily.

I held out a farthing. "You're to deliver this to the surgeon, Mr Goodchild – you can remember the address I told you? Just behind the cricket ground." He took the coin and nodded. "And there'll be another farthing for you from Mr Goodchild, so make sure you give it direct to him." His heels given wings by the promise of a half-penny before noon, Daniel raced off and I settled myself to waiting. I had done all I could in preparation.

Patience is one of the signal characteristics of the police constable, but I will confess that it comes easier to me now in later years than it did at the beginning. As a young officer I was quick to judge and quick to act. Ironic, isn't it: when you're young and have plenty of time you're always in a hurry, but as it runs out, you learn to pause, to consider and reflect. Things are almost never what they seem at first look: the painted trollop winking at gentlemen in Regent Street is no more than a child, and the fine coach-horse offered for sale with boot-black on its hooves is ready for the knackers. So I've learnt to take the time to let things reveal themselves. If you sit, quiet and patient, oftentimes the bird will come to you. But chase it and call out, trying to catch it, and off it flies.

So I was less irritated than I might once have been, given that I had already spent the whole of the previous evening waiting outside the bank in Berners Street. But Mr Fauntleroy had not come back to his house next door to the bank, and so eventually I had posted my deputy to stand watch until the morning and gone back to Mrs Plank in the early hours for a bit of home comfort and a rest. I'd tried to lift the bedcovers and get in without waking her, but a constable's wife knows not to sleep deep until her man is home and beside her, and she drew my arm across her and pulled me in close, sharing her warmth.

A good woman, Martha, although she never could understand why I do the work I do. "Why didn't you stay a barber?" she'd ask. "It's steady work – whiskers always grow. And you'd be home nights."

But barbering was just a youthful diversion, and by the time I was waiting for Henry Fauntleroy I had been a constable for twenty-five years, wearing my blue frock coat and top hat with pride. Taking Martha's advice – or, truth be told, her drunken father's – I had tried the Redbreast life for a few months, as part of the foot patrol working out of Bow Street. "Good money, that," said the old bugger, looking out for his daughter and even more for his own fondness for the ale. "Sell your services to whoever pays the most, and a bounty for every arrest." And he wasn't wrong: a good Runner could earn proper money – up to seventy pounds if his catch made it all the way to the scaffold. And many of them added to their pay with, well, let's call them donations from a grateful public. But I'd also seen the way the crowd could turn on these

mercenaries, ignoring their hue and cry for help, scream-
ing abuse at them, and obstructing them in their pursuit
of a popular local villain. And to my mind, swaggering
round in a red waistcoat and swinging a gilt-topped cane
was poor recompense for all of that.

I flatter myself that over the years I built myself a good
reputation as a constable, at Great Marlborough Street
and beyond. I tended to get the best business: if a case
required tact or delicacy – both sadly lacking in some
younger constables – it would be passed to me to decide
who to assign. I'll be the first to admit that I'm not the
strongest or the fleetest of men, but brute force and speed
are easy to come by, and I always made sure that I had at
least one strapping young constable within sound of my
whistle.

And so that's how I came to be in charge of the Fauntleroy arrest. It was always going to be a sensitive case,
with the banker being a close friend of several magistrates. And as a man of means, he might even attempt to
bribe his way out of it, so the arresting officer needed to
be above temptation – or at least, temptation of the mon-
etary kind. Lord, if I'd taken one tenth of the bribes offered to me to wink at the escape of some wealthy or titled
culprit, I might have retired years ago with a handsome
fortune.

After a good breakfast and a pinch of Martha's ample backside at which she pretended outrage, I put on my coat and walked to Great Marlborough Street. I always found it invigorating to see the metropolis come to life around me, imagining myself as one small cog in the great machine of London. Waiting outside the police office was a gang of lads – the regulars, always on hand to run messages or shadow a suspect. One spotted me and came over with a note that stated simply: "He is returned."

Seasoned constable though I was, my blood still quickened at the prospect of an arrest, and I fairly trotted down the road. But once I reached Berners Street I slowed my pace so as not to attract attention, and walked seemingly casually past the bank at number six. I then crossed the road to observe the imposing double front door from a safe distance. My deputy – a handy fellow called William Wilson – was waiting a little further down the street, and nodded slightly in acknowledgement without looking at me, just as I had taught him.

A few minutes later the surgeon John Goodchild appeared, puffing slightly from his brisk walk and pulling at his collar. He hesitated at the steps to the bank and would have gone in had I not coughed to catch his attention and beckoned him over the road. Goodchild was a man of quiet dress and habits, a gentle and unassuming soul, and obviously ill at ease with his role this day.

"So, constable," he said, "here I am." He blinked rapidly and covered a yawn. "Forgive me: I did not sleep well. Concerned about today."

"I am sorry to hear that, sir," I replied. "But you do remember our rehearsal yesterday; you know what you are to do?"

Goodchild nodded, but he was pale. "So he is in there?" he asked.

"Mr Fauntleroy arrived about an hour ago," I confirmed. I laid a hand on the surgeon's shoulder, seeking to calm him. "I know it's frightening to confront a man like this," I continued. "Like animals, people can be unpredictable when they're cornered. But I will be following you shortly, and Constable Wilson is just over there. And we must go in now, sir, or we will miss our chance. Are you ready?"

Goodchild swallowed hard. "As ready as I'll ever be." He waited until a hackney had passed before crossing back towards the bank. At the top of the steps he turned to look at me, and I smiled to reassure him. He wiped his palms on his jacket and pushed open the door.

According to the later testimony of the chief clerk, Goodchild crossed the tiled floor, black and white in the pattern of a chessboard, his heels ringing on the hard surface. He walked up to the mahogany desk in the middle of the room and spoke to the young clerk sitting there.

"I should like to see Mr Fauntleroy, please. It is a matter of some urgency concerning the Bellis will. My name is Goodchild."

Exactly as we had practised. The clerk looked up from his ledger and laid down his pen. He indicated a chair where Goodchild could wait and disappeared behind the banking counter, returning shortly to escort the visitor into the banker's office.

Two minutes later, I entered the banking hall and went to the main banking counter. I presented a cheque for cashing to the chief clerk, an older man with a balding head and a look of weariness. The cheque had been helpfully provided by a tradesman round the corner who owed me a favour; more than once I had protected his shop from light-fingered visitors. As the clerk busied himself with the cheque, inspecting it carefully and then transcribing its details into his large banking ledger, I glanced to my left. Through the half-glazed door, I could see the back of Goodchild's head and – over his shoulder and seated opposite him – the banker Fauntleroy. Content now that my quarry was on the premises and unlikely to make a run for it, and ignoring the indignant and ineffectual protests of both clerks, I walked smartly past the banking counter and made for the banker's office. Alerted by the clerks' cries, the banker leapt to his feet, but it was too late: I was in his office and had shut the door behind me.

The hunted look in the banker's eyes told me plainer than any evidence that I had found my man, and I held out the arrest warrant. He stared at it but did not reach out to take it, and so I let it fall onto the desk between us, where it unfolded slightly to reveal the seal of John Conant. Seeing the name of one of his friends seemed to startle Fauntleroy into a reaction.

"Good God!" he cried. "Cannot this business be settled?" He pulled open the top drawer of his desk and took out his cheque book. With a shaking hand, he turned to a blank cheque and held his pen poised above it, the tremor of his grip spattering tiny drops of ink onto the paper. He looked up at me.

"I'm afraid not, sir," I said. Even though I had half-expected it, it was still sad to see a supposed man of honour betray himself. "Are you Mr Henry Fauntleroy, senior partner of this bank?"

Fauntleroy nodded and collapsed into his chair, his pen falling with a clatter onto the desk. Goodchild, doubtless relieved that his part was done, likewise subsided.

"The keys to the safe, please, sir," I said, holding out my hand. Fauntleroy reached into the drawer again, unclipped a secret compartment, pulled out a bunch of keys and put them on the desk. "And the key to your desk too, if you please, sir," I added as I picked them up. Fauntleroy hesitated, and then pulled his watch from its pocket and detached from its chain a small brass key, which he handed to me. I put all of the keys carefully into an inside pocket of my jacket. "Mr Goodchild," I said without letting my eyes leave the banker's face. "Please observe that I have taken these keys from Mr Fauntleroy and am putting them into this pocket."

I opened the office door. The clerks were standing where I had left them, mouths open with astonishment, watched by Wilson who had taken up his position by the entrance. "Lock the door behind us when we leave, Wilson," I instructed him. "No-one is to come in, and no-one is to leave. No-one," I repeated as one of the clerks drew breath to object. "Mr Fauntleroy and Mr Goodchild are coming with me." I stood back to let the two gentlemen precede me, and the three of us walked through the banking hall and out of the front door. Behind us the lock fell shut as Wilson secured the premises.

We walked in silence down the steps of the bank and turned left, my hand steering the banker lightly by the elbow. Berners Street was quiet at that time of day; the gentlemen of leisure who frequented its premises were rarely about before midday. But when we joined Oxford Street it was another story and people crowded in on us from all sides. Carts carrying produce from the farms in the west to sell in the capital streamed past in an unbroken flow. Newspaper boys cried the titles of their rival publications, each trying to out-yell the competition. Pie-men with steaming trays on their heads called out prices – had I been alone, I would have been tempted. Fauntle-roy stopped, almost stunned, and I took his arm to steady him. Not that I thought that the banker would run. No, I had seen his face when I presented the warrant and I knew what it meant. After ten years of looking over his shoulder, of jumping at every unexpected caller, of living with the daily expectation of capture and exposure, Fauntleroy would not want to add to that tally. We ne-gotiated our way across the road, ducked down Argyll Street and finally turned into Great Marlborough Street.

# CHAPTER TWO

# The reluctant magistrate

## FRIDAY 10<sup>TH</sup> SEPTEMBER 1824

I doubt Fauntleroy was in any state to notice it, but it was generous and delicate of the magistrate to allow us to avoid the public entrance to the court. Instead, John Conant – who, like many of his profession, lived above the shop – received us in his private residence. Following the footman who had answered my knock, we climbed the narrow staircase from the side entrance to the building and filed into the magistrate's dining room. Conant and Fauntleroy were acquainted socially, and I had seen as he had signed the arrest warrant the previous day that the magistrate was very sorry to see the banker brought before him in this way. Extending one long, thin hand of welcome to Fauntleroy, Conant gestured with the other to the most comfortable of the chairs in the room. Goodchild shrank into another seat against the wall, trying to fade into the wallpaper, while I declined a third: I always find that I am most alert and observant while standing.

I liked Conant. Unlike some magistrates he took his work seriously, and was as incorruptible as I was myself. He was the son of the famous and respected magistrate Sir Nathaniel Conant, and like many sons of famous fathers had struggled to make his own mark. A portrait of his late father looked down on our gathering that afternoon with distaste and disappointment – or maybe it was just poor brushwork by the artist. The son was an altogether leaner figure than his large-girthed father, with more delicate features and the upright carriage common to Navy men.

The footman had just brought coffee when a man announced as John Hume joined us. Like Goodchild he was a trustee of the Bellis will, and it was their discovery of the loss of the Bellis funds that had brought us all to this point. Two clerks of the court slipped in silently and sat at either end of the dining table, their books open before them in readiness for note-taking. Last to arrive were George Graham, introduced for the benefit of those notes as one of the partners in Fauntleroy's banking house, and three of their clerks – the two who had witnessed the arrest and one other whom I had not seen before. Their hats clutched nervously in their hands, the three clerks formed a straggling crow-like row along one wall, there being no more seats left to accommodate them.

Mr Conant started with words so familiar to me that I could recite them in my head like the creed on Sundays. "This is not a trial," he explained. "This is an initial hearing, to establish the basis of the public examination that is to come, when lawyers for and against will argue their case in court."

He then started to gather information. I could guess many of the questions and most of the answers, and so I concentrated instead on watching the banker. A man gives himself away not just with his words but also with his face and his body. Fauntleroy sat small in his chair, both hands holding his hat tightly in his lap except when one or other was nervously smoothing down his hair. On and on went the questions, the corroboration of answers, the clarification for the record. The pens of the clerks scratched across their books, their fingers becoming ever more stained with the ink as they dipped their nibs again and again. At one point, Fauntleroy cried out in a strained and cracking voice, "I alone am guilty! My partners did not know." Graham exhaled a sigh of relief at this, but still the questioning went on. The bank clerks and I shifted as our feet started to ache.

After nearly two hours, Mr Conant had heard enough. He rose from his chair, sighed and said, "I am satisfied that

there is a case to answer, that the banker Henry Fauntleroy should be examined further on this matter. The date
for the public examination is set for..." He looked questioningly at one of the court clerks, who consulted a large
ledger, wrote a date on a scrap of paper and handed it to
Conant. The magistrate continued. "The public examination will take place here, at Great Marlborough Street
Magistrates' Court, on Saturday the eighteenth of September, at four o'clock. Yes, Mr Fauntleroy – what is it?"

The banker cleared his throat. "The week from now
until then, Mr Conant – will I be permitted to return to
the bank to ensure that things will run smoothly in my
absence? Or will I have to spend the time at home? My
partners know something of the current business at the
bank..." His voice trailed off as the magistrate and I exchanged glances. I felt almost sorry for the banker, who
had plainly failed to grasp the seriousness of his situation.

"Mr Fauntleroy, I quite understand your desire to attend to matters both professional and personal," said Mr
Conant with genuine sadness, "but the gravity of the offence of which you are accused leaves me no option but
to commit you to custody until the hearing."

One of his clerks handed him a sheet of paper, and the
magistrate leaned forward to sign it. His hand shook very
slightly. A dedicated and efficient magistrate, Mr Conant
had sent scores of men, women and even children to gaol,
but I suspect that few of his decisions had disquieted him

as much as this one. Conant handed the warrant back to the clerk, who checked it and passed it to me. I did not look at it; I had been a policeman long enough to know its contents.

"Mr Fauntleroy," said the magistrate, "that warrant instructs Constable Plank to accompany you to the house of correction at Coldbath Fields. There you will be detained until you are brought back to this court in a week's time. Might I suggest that you use that time to consult a lawyer and prepare your defence."

I watched the banker's reaction to the name of the prison. He went a little paler but, like a child remembering his mother's instructions to be polite, he took care to shake the hand of the magistrate and thank him for his hospitality.

At the door of the dining room, Fauntleroy stopped and spoke to the clerk I had not recognised, laying his hand upon the man's arm. The clerk, several inches taller than the banker, put his hand over that of his master, and bent his head to hear him. I turned away, seeming to give them privacy, but actually listening very closely.

"Tyson," said Fauntleroy, "would you be good enough to call in on my mother when you return to the bank, and let her know that I have been detained. Tell her only that there has been a misunderstanding at the bank and that I am helping to unravel it – pray do not mention Coldbath, but say merely that I will be away from home for a few nights. I will send for my brother John: he is an attorney and will know what to do. And get word of my arrest to Freddy Lampton – his address is in the green book on my desk. Lampton – don't forget."

I stood impassively – but I would make a note of that name later. I led the banker down the stairs and checked that Wilson had secured a hackney coach before we went out into the street. When he saw us, Wilson opened the door of the hackney and climbed in. I indicated that Fauntleroy should go in next, and I followed him. As I stepped in behind the banker, I glanced back over my shoulder and saw the magistrate at his dining room window looking down at us. He shook his head before turning away. Just then one of the court clerks appeared at the door of the coach and handed me a sealed note.

"For Mr Vickery, from Mr Conant. Urgent," he said.

I slammed the door and we set off.

We rode in silence from Great Marlborough Street eastwards, then the hackney turned north, barging its way across the busy thoroughfare of Oxford Street before heading east again to Clerkenwell, right to the very edge of the city. Wilson shivered as the bulk of the house of correction loomed up alongside us.

"So much for a cold bath being good for the health!" he said almost to himself. I shot him a warning look and he said no more.

Coldbath Fields certainly had a fearsome reputation, and even regular visitors were unnerved by it. It was a massive, squat group of red-brick buildings surrounding eight large exercise yards, with small barred windows high in the walls providing the only light to the hundreds of apartments within. I was once told that the original house of correction had been designed by a man who had spent years in a terrible French gaol and came home fired with a passion for reform, designing prisons with areas for inmates to get exercise and fresh air. However, as more people fell from the path of righteousness and as Middlesex's magistrates demanded space for the detention of an ever-increasing number of miscreants, Coldbath lapsed from that ideal and by the time I delivered Fauntleroy to its doors, it was a crowded, filthy and brutal place.

As far as I could see, its only saving grace was its keeper, John Vickery. A former Bow Street Runner, Vickery was a good man – honest and compassionate. Working with criminals can turn a man one of two ways: either he becomes worse than the worst criminal himself, or he learns that there is nearly always a reason for a man to turn bad. Perhaps he has been treated harshly by others, or maybe he has too many mouths to feed and not enough skill to do it, or perhaps he cannot see that others are using him to do their dirty work. So you learn not to judge a person until you know why, as well as what, when and how.

When the hackney came to a halt, I left Fauntleroy and Wilson inside while I jumped down and bade one of the two gatekeepers to fetch John Vickery. A tall, well-built man with a full head of red hair, the keeper came within minutes and I handed him the arrest warrant, which formally stated the charge on which Fauntleroy was to be imprisoned: having feloniously forged and uttered as true a certain instrument with intention to defraud the Governor and Company of the Bank of England. I also gave him the sealed note from the magistrate, which he opened and read before showing it to me. The note said, "Keep this man in your safest custody – protect him from all including himself". Vickery raised his eyebrows at me before approaching the hackney.

From my conversations with the turnkeys, I knew that sixteen of the apartments in Coldbath Fields had no window to the outside world. These most secure of cells were completely surrounded by other cells, their only light coming from a small aperture above the door. It was to one of these dark, dank, hidden apartments that Vickery led the banker and me, along with two turnkeys. The smell of the prison was familiar to me – a mixture of damp, filth, waste and fear – but Fauntleroy shrank from the stench and at one point whipped out a handkerchief to cover his nose and mouth and contain his retching. I had done the same on my first visit.

Seven feet wide by ten feet deep, the cell was secured by a thick oak door. Its only furniture was a wooden table with two chairs, a wash-hand basin on a stool, and a stump bedstead. Yet when Vickery led Fauntleroy into the cell, the banker seemed to recover himself. He thanked Vickery as graciously as if he had been shown to a fireside seat in his club, and made no objection when Vickery indicated to one of the turnkeys to stay in the tiny cell with the prisoner.

It was time for me to leave. "Farewell, sir," I said to the banker. "Until next week."

"Next week?" he repeated.

"Indeed, sir: I am to accompany you to the hearing next Saturday – a week tomorrow."

"I daresay I shall be glad to see a familiar face, constable." And he smiled weakly.

Outside the cell, Vickery instructed the other turnkey to lock the door and to sit nearby, ready to swap shifts with the man inside, so that Fauntleroy would spend his first night in gaol under the unwavering gaze of Vickery's men.

"Why do you think a man like that does such a thing, constable?" Vickery asked me as we made their way back to the front of the prison. "A man with position and wealth, to risk it all. Is it the daring of the thing? A grand wager?"

I shook my head. "Sometimes, yes, sir, but not this time, I don't think," I said. "He's not a man made for reckless excitement. He did it, of that I'm certain; I've never seen a man act more guilty. But why? That's where the interest of it will lie, I'm sure."

CHAPTER THREE

# A most unpleasant man

## TUESDAY 14ᵀᴴ SEPTEMBER 1824

The following Tuesday I had just arrived at Great Marlborough Street when one of the younger officers waylaid me.

"You're wanted upstairs," he said, jerking his head in the direction of Mr Conant's apartment. "Right away, he said."

Another delicate arrest, I assumed as I climbed the stairs to the magistrate's dining room. I knocked lightly on the door and he called me in; he had just finished his breakfast and was readying himself for a day on the bench by sorting through various papers. I stood and waited, fully expecting him to pass me a warrant, but he did not. Instead, he waved me towards a chair opposite his own,

21

and I sat rather uneasily – this was obviously going to be a serious discussion.

"Constable Plank," he began, and then stopped. "Constable Plank," he tried again, "what do you know of Mr Fauntleroy, from Friday last?"

I was surprised by his question but answered as fully as I could. "I know that he is suspected of forgery concerning assets held in trust under the Bellis will, and that you were worried enough about his state of mind to send a note of warning to the keeper at Coldbath."

"And how did he – Fauntleroy I mean – seem to you, constable? At the arrest, and afterwards?"

"Seem to me, sir?"

Mr Conant leaned forward in his seat. "Did you think him guilty, Plank?"

It was rare for a magistrate to concern himself with the opinions of one of his officers. I recalled my conversation with Vickery, and wondered whether he had relayed it to the magistrate. But he had asked and so I answered him truthfully. "Yes, sir, I did." He made no reply, so I continued. "He offered me a bribe, sir, which I generally take as a sign of guilt. But not just that: when I arrested him, he seemed almost relieved to have been caught."

Mr Conant sat back in his chair. "So you saw that too? I wondered if it was my imagination." He stood up and walked to the window, looking unseeingly down into the street. "Do you think he acted alone, constable? Or are there others involved?"

"Mr Graham, you mean, sir? His partner at the bank?"

The magistrate shook his head. "Unlikely, to my mind. I wondered more about that tall clerk of his, or perhaps someone helping him to sell the Bellis stock..." He turned to look at me. "You have an interest in forgery, don't you, Plank? I recall that you were concerned in the prosecution of Philip Whitehead."

I nodded. "That was some time ago, sir – in 1812."

The magistrate continued. "A long-standing interest, then, constable. What I need is someone to make discreet enquiries about Mr Fauntleroy and his bank. Word will be out by now that he is under arrest, and if we are not careful, anyone else who is involved will cover their tracks and disappear. We need to act swiftly but carefully, Plank. Take whatever time you need; I leave it to you."

I was able to start my enquiries even sooner than Mr Conant could have hoped. The moment I returned to the police office, George Cooper beckoned me over.

"Thank goodness you're here, Sam," he said. "I've got one here who's determined to have his say. He's a gentleman and I don't want to lock him in the cells, but if he doesn't settle himself down he's headed that way."

George Cooper had been the gaoler at Great Marlborough Street ever since it had opened more than thirty years earlier, and a more patient man never walked this earth. Gaolers in other police offices would throw you into a cell soon as look at you, leaving you to stew in your own juice until you sobered up or came to your senses, while George preferred to give a person the benefit of the doubt. But I could tell that the ruddy-faced man who turned to look at me when he heard my name had just about run out of benefit.

"Sam? Constable Samuel Plank?" he bellowed.

"Take him into the back room and sort him out," said George with a wink. "I've cleared out the night visitors, so there'll be space in the cells if you decide you need it after all."

In the tiny room at the back of the police office, with its frosted window overlooking the yard, I indicated that my visitor should sit in one of the four chairs crowded around the small table. When he did not, I sat down myself, and took out my notebook. I waited while he considered, gnawing on his lip now and then, his hands jammed into his pockets. Under the prominent red veins so typical of a heavy drinker, he had the sun-darkened skin of someone who lived in a place rather warmer than London. And he wore too many clothes, as though he felt the cold – his blood thinned perhaps from years in a tropical climate. He finally thrust out a hand for me to shake.

"Robert Harvey, of St Kitts."

"Constable Samuel Plank," I responded. "How can I help you, Mr Harvey?"

He dropped into the chair opposite me. "My sister is Marianne Fauntleroy, married to that blackguard – well, when I say married to, more like abandoned by him, the swine. Took a dear, sweet, innocent girl and contaminated her with his filthy..." His face grew redder.

"Mr Harvey," I held up my hand. "Perhaps you can explain precisely why you wanted to see me. Are you and your sister injured parties in the allegations of fraud against the bank?"

Harvey snorted. "Injured parties? Not in financial terms, no – we Harveys have always been smart enough with money, and thankfully our father saw to it that Marianne's inheritance was put beyond the reach of any fortune-seeking husband. Just as well, given what I've been hearing – the bank's on the verge of collapse, they say, thanks to his thieving. But this Fauntleroy's a slippery fellow, and no doubt he'll be finding all sorts of high-ups to speak in his defence, to say that he's an honest chap."

"And you think different?"

"So will you, once you hear my side of things."

I opened my notebook.

"It was not long after he took over the bank, after his father died," began Harvey. "Youngest managing partner in London – pah!"

"So this was 1808?" I tried to remember what I had read about Fauntleroy's banking house.

"The old man died in March 1807, and Fauntleroy got his hands on the lot the very next day. Convinced the other partners – a farmer from Norfolk and some society fool – that he would be a good replacement for his father. Well, they know better now, don't they?"

I thought back to George Graham's shattered look in the magistrate's dining room but didn't venture an opinion.

"Anyway, my sister and I were in England in the summer of 1808, visiting the family and – let's not be coy about it – looking for a suitable husband for Marianne. St Kitts offers limited society, and at twenty-three she was running out of options. The Fauntleroys were friends of friends; over the season we met him on several occasions, and he showed Marianne some preference. I wasn't taken with him myself – a bit too insipid for me, looked like a sea voyage would kill him – but Marianne was keen."

"And so a wedding was planned?" I asked.

"Planned?" he said with a bark of laughter. "Demanded, more like. Required, if you see my meaning." I nodded. "Turns out that Marianne and the blackguard had taken a ride in a curricle one evening, unchaperoned – he'd convinced her that it would be a lark. And silly girl, she fell for the romance of it all, and with the two of them alone, and her unused to the attentions of men – well, you can imagine. But damn it, Plank: a gentleman would not have done it. Give me the plain slave any day: he is what he is, and doesn't pretend to be a gentleman while acting like a beast. Anyway, Marianne eventually told our mother what had happened and it became clear that Fauntleroy would have to marry her. And so I went round to his bank one evening to confront him, waiting until everyone else had left.

"He came to the door with a glass in his hand – so much for his professed religious sensibilities about strong drink. And I made it clear to him that in my opinion a gentleman would have waited to make good on the deal before taking the prize. He didn't seem to understand, so I had to spell it out. 'Marianne is with child,' I said. 'Your child.' Well, that sank in. He went completely white, the milksop, and collapsed into a chair. I started to talk of a wedding, and – can you believe it? – he seemed to think that there might be an alternative. Keeping my sister as another one of his women, I suppose. But he soon changed his mind when I mentioned my duelling pistols."

Harvey smirked at the memory, and I could clearly see the bully in him.

"If you were prepared to fight a duel, I take it you were planning to leave England?" I asked.

"Good God, yes – nothing could tempt me to stay in this damp, dreary place a minute longer than necessary. Once I saw Marianne safely married, I intended to get back to my plantation. My mother had to stay behind, of course, to be with Marianne and the child. I think Mother and I both knew that he would be of no practical help." He punched one hand lightly into the other.

"The wedding?" I prompted.

"Well, when he realised that there was no way out, there was a ceremony of sorts that summer – the sixteenth of July, 1809. Not far from here: St Pancras Church. I gave my sister away – with a heavy heart, as you can imagine. Then we went back to Fauntleroy's house, next door to the bank, but after only an hour none of us could keep up the pretence of a celebration any longer, and so Marianne and my mother set off for Tunbridge Wells."

"Tunbridge Wells?"

"Yes: Fauntleroy had taken a house there for them – safely tucked away from his life in London. Didn't want a wife and baby interfering with his drinking parties and gaming, did he? Anyway, before I left for Southampton I needed to settle the matter of money with him, and so I bearded him in his den. I laid down a few ground rules, making it clear that Marianne was to be his wife in name only, and that all visits to my sister and the child would be with my permission."

"And Mr Fauntleroy agreed to this?"

"No objection at all; as I say, he was glad to see the back of her. I gave him the name of our solicitor – Mr Tobias

Anderson – and said that he would handle all arrangements. The story that Anderson and I had agreed was that as far as the good folk of Tunbridge Wells were to be concerned, Mrs Marianne Fauntleroy was the loving wife of the successful London banker Henry Fauntleroy. Her delicate health prevented her from living in London with him, and his business responsibilities prevented him from visiting her on a frequent basis. The pretence of delicate health would also explain the early arrival of the child, should there be any comment on the matter, and our widowed mother would be her companion.

"With regard to money, I had done some calculations and told Fauntleroy that I expected him to give Marianne an allowance of three hundred and fifty pounds, payable each year on the anniversary of their marriage. And here's a funny thing. He said that he disagreed. I was outraged: I knew him to be a liar and a libertine, but I had not thought that he was tight-fisted as well. I started to remonstrate with him but he interrupted and said that he disagreed because it was not enough. He wanted to pay four hundred. Have you ever heard such a thing? And they call him canny with money!" Harvey shook his head and laughed disbelievingly.

I smiled but made no comment. In Fauntleroy's shoes, I too might have thought it fifty pounds well spent to wipe the pompous smirk off this man's face. "And the child?" I asked.

"A boy, born three months later. Henry, like his father. We'll have to change that now, of course – he can't spend the rest of his life with that cursed name, once his father goes to the gallows."

"And is that why you have come to me today, Mr Harvey?" I asked. "To add your voice to those who wish to see your brother-in-law hang?"

Perhaps he heard the disapproval in my question.

"All I ask, Constable Plank," he said, much on his dignity, "is that my evidence as to Henry Fauntleroy's character – that of a man who takes advantage of an innocent young woman and then abandons her – is put into the balance against all of the society buffoons who will doubtless leap to his defence."

# CHAPTER FOUR

# Napoleon's tent

## THURSDAY 16TH SEPTEMBER 1824

Other matters conspired to take my attention during the week following Fauntleroy's arrest, but I could not concentrate on any of them and instead found my thoughts returning again and again to the banker. The image of him – dressed in his sombre suit, with his manicured nails and withdrawn manner, sitting in that pitiful cell – played on my mind. His calmness bothered me; apart from his initial outburst, when he had tried to buy me off, he had not railed against his fate. In my experience, only two types of men are so accepting of arrest and incarceration: those who have struggled with concealing their guilt and almost welcome the exposure, and those who already have a plan for escape. But which was Fauntleroy?

I needed to know more about him, to satisfy my own curiosity as well as for Mr Conant, and there are few better ways to get the measure of a man than to see where he spends his private hours. I had no wish to meet Fauntleroy's mother or sister, or to explain to them my interest in his rooms, so I told Wilson to wait outside their house until he saw the ladies leave to make social calls, as I felt certain they would.

And indeed a note from Wilson was delivered to me at the police office at just gone ten on the Thursday morning, and I hurried to the Fauntleroy home in Berners Street. I knocked on the door, and told the wide-eyed maid that I was a policeman acting on instructions from the magistrate, and that she was to show me to her master's study and there leave me in peace. She led me into a lofty entrance hall and pointed to one of several tall, dark doors leading off it. I went into Fauntleroy's study and shut the door firmly in the maid's face.

Even without knowing Fauntleroy, I could have guessed from this room that he was a man of business rather than leisure. Tin boxes were stacked neatly on the shelves, each carefully labelled. I peered into one or two and they were filled with papers. The desk was clear, the blotter and pens lined up in expectation of work, and on the table beside the armchair was a single volume with a bookmark about halfway through. I picked it up and turned to the title page: *The Pilot: A Tale of the Sea* by Fenimore Cooper. The rest of the room was not Spartan exactly, but spare – everything seemed to have a purpose, with the furniture solid and serviceable rather than showy. The only purely decorative item was on the mantelpiece: a bust of Napoleon, about eight inches high, gazed out across the study. I picked it up and the alabaster was cool and heavy in my hands. I am no expert on such things, but it seemed to me to be a good likeness, competently executed. And very out of place for an Englishman.

To one side of the fireplace was another door – smaller and probably leading to a private chamber. I turned the knob gingerly, half-expecting the door to be locked, but it opened outwards. It was obstructed by a curtain hanging across it on the far side, so I reached through to pull it aside and stepped into – well, I hardly know how to describe it. The contrast with the study was marked. It was, I suppose, a billiard room, with a fine table on a Brussels carpet in the centre of it and an array of cues in a stand against the wall. But the curtain across the door was only the start of it. Every wall was draped with matching hangings, in a rich purple silk, and even the ceiling was swagged in the same material, caught up in the centre by a chandelier. The effect was of standing inside a magnificent and extravagant tent.

As I backed out of the billiard room, it struck me that the contrast between the restrained furnishings of the banker's study and the flamboyance of the purple tent could not have been more marked. How much more of Fauntleroy's true nature was hidden away behind closed doors?

# CHAPTER FIVE

# Calming the creditors

## SATURDAY 18ᵀᴴ SEPTEMBER 1824

The following Saturday promised to be busy. First there was a meeting for creditors of Fauntleroy's bank, and at the end of the afternoon the banker himself would be attending a second hearing. I intended to use both opportunities to find out more about the man and his motives.

The Boar and Castle at the east end of Oxford Street was not an inn I visited regularly – or at least, not when out of uniform and off-duty. No policeman wants to drink in a place where he is likely to stand elbow to elbow with someone he has arrested in the past. But that is where the anonymous advertisements in the newspapers had said that the creditors would be meeting, and so I left my frock coat and top hat at the police office, borrowed something more anonymous from the store-room, and made sure to arrive just before one o'clock, the advertised time for the meeting.

The place was already busy, which suited me as I could slip in at the back without drawing attention to myself. I was worried about taking notes, but there were so many others doing so – newspapermen, I guessed, and perhaps angry customers and their solicitors – that I did not look out of place when I took out my notebook. Folded up in it was the bankruptcy notice that I had torn out of the *Morning Chronicle* two days earlier, and I read it again. "Bankruptcy of Messrs Marsh and Company – The creditors are requested forthwith to send in their Banking Books to the House in Berners Street, for the purpose of their being made up by the Clerks acting under the Provisional Assignees appointed by the Commissioners." Doubtless many of those attending today had read the same notice, and wanted to find out more before contacting the assignees by the given deadline at the end of the month.

I estimated that there were just over fifty of us squeezed into the room. No-one seemed to know who had arranged the meeting; several people called out to ask who was in charge, but no-one answered. At ten past the hour, a thin, greying man stood up and said that his name was John Frost, and that we had all come to the meeting with the same purpose: to find out what was to happen to our holdings at the bank of Marsh and Company. And just when I was thinking that he was our chairman, he said, "And now it is time for whoever called this meeting to make himself known to us." We all looked around, trying to catch each other's eye without letting our own be caught.

Then the crowd parted and a small, round man in an apron was pushed to the front.

"I am William Sanderson," he said, wiping his hands nervously on a cloth. "Landlord here. And I have upwards of five hundred pounds at the bank in question. Along with two other local merchants – Mr Marks and Mr Allen – I called this meeting. But I am no speaker. Perhaps Mr Frost would be willing to take charge?" Frost agreed, saying that although he had no agenda prepared, he would chair the meeting and make sure that all were heard. There was a show of hands, including my own, and he was appointed.

Frost first asked if anyone had anything in particular to say. A tall man with a great bushy beard stood up; Charters, he said his name was, from the distillery Holland and Company in Lewisham, and that he was here to find a way to obtain possession of our property, as he put it. This went down well, and there was a chorus of "Hear, hear!"

The landlord Sanderson whispered something in Frost's ear, and the chairman nodded. He told us that a message had been sent to the bank, asking for a representative to attend the meeting. "Is there anyone here representing Marsh and Company?" he called out. No-one replied. This did not surprise me: after all, Fauntleroy was in Coldbath, and none of the other directors was involved enough in the daily business of the bank to be able to answer any questions. And I think Frost knew it too; when someone called out "Shame!", the chairman held up a calming hand and said (and I noted this carefully), "At the present moment, we have no reason to doubt that Marsh and Company have cash in the house sufficient to pay all who have claims upon them". He also warned the crowd that any rash measures they might take could throw the estate into the hands of what he called improper persons, with the result that any property would be swallowed up in legal proceedings. I confess, I liked Frost more and more – and was grateful that he was there to balance the hotheads.

One such stood up and suggested that the property might already be gone – "Fauntleroy's taken the lot!" he yelled, his mottled cheeks quivering with anger. And I had read similar outraged accusations in the paper that very morning, so he was not alone in thinking this. But again, Frost's level approach calmed the crowd. He explained that although the full extent of the forgeries was as yet unknown, as regards the known forgeries on the Bank of England, the creditors of the bank should not be affected – that, according to law, creditors of a partnership have priority over creditors of the individual partners. And the Bank of England was a creditor of Henry Fauntleroy – not of the banking partnership – and so stood in the queue behind creditors of the bank. No wonder people need lawyers to make sense of it all.

"All I want to know," called out another man once Frost had stopped speaking, "is whether my money is safe." Everyone went quiet, waiting for Frost to answer, and he paused to choose his words. Eventually he said (and again, I was careful to note it exactly), "Until it is ascertained that the bank itself is not affected by Mr Fauntleroy's operations, it is premature to pronounce, from mere appearances, what will fall to the share of the creditors." His measured tone seemed to reassure his audience that they now knew as much as there was to know, and the meeting broke up peaceably soon afterwards.

I have often noted that men of all classes – no matter how grand their houses, no matter how fancy their clothes – react in the same way to adversity. They gather together in crowds, they seek a scapegoat, they look to someone to provide comfort and calm and reassurance. And if all victims are the same, what about the perpetrators – are they too essentially the same? Was Henry

Fauntleroy simply a common thief with a fine wardrobe and a good education?

# CHAPTER SIX

# Four depositions

## SATURDAY 18TH SEPTEMBER 1824

The sky darkened in the early afternoon, and by the time we drew up outside Coldbath Fields at just gone three o'clock, rain was lashing the windows of the hackney. I pulled my coat collar tight around my neck as I walked swiftly to the entrance, leaving Wilson in the shelter of the coach. Never run, I had been told when I started out in uniform, and it was a rule I passed on to young constables. A running police officer spreads panic or – worse – looks scared.

The prison gate opened, and there stood John Vickery, punctual as always, with Henry Fauntleroy at his side. The banker was not as dapper as when I had last seen him, but his shirt was clean and he had managed to shave leaving only a few small cuts. I handed Vickery the warrant transferring temporary responsibility for his prisoner to me, and took the banker by the elbow. Fauntleroy stopped halfway to the hackney, and turned his face to the sky. "Rain!" he said in wonderment, as he let it run down his cheeks.

As we journeyed to the court, the banker took a great deal of interest in his surroundings, craning his neck to see past me and Wilson and out of the windows. A few days locked away will certainly make a man appreciate the world.

"Will it be a similar arrangement to last time?" he asked me. "In Mr Conant's rooms at Great Marlborough Street?"

"Ah, no," I said. "That was a more informal initial hearing. Today is what is called a public examination – didn't your lawyer explain that to you? Mr Harmer, isn't it?" Being on friendly terms with most of the court clerks meant that I generally knew which lawyer was working for whom.

"Yes, Mr Harmer. And he did," said Fauntleroy, "but I suppose I was hoping that he might be wrong – that Mr Conant might be able to, well, keep the crowds away."

"I'm afraid not, sir," I said. "It is a public hearing, so Mr Conant cannot keep the crowds away. And there are indeed crowds."

Avoiding the crush at the main entrance in Great Marlborough Street, I led Fauntleroy down a passageway, up the back stairs to the court and into an antechamber. He walked to one side of the window, made sure that he was hidden by the curtain, and looked down into the street.

"Who are all these people?" he asked. "What are they to do with my case?"

I caught Wilson's eye, and he went to look at the pushing and shoving throng battling its way up the steps of the building. "They're what we call interested parties, sir," he said. "I understand that some of them are creditors of the bank, who want to know whether their money is safe – apparently there's no-one answering their questions in Berners Street, so they've come here instead." It was the most I had ever heard Wilson say, and it made perfect sense. Usually these young constables were more muscle than anything, but perhaps this one had a mind too.

"They can't all be creditors," said Fauntleroy in disbelief. "Our banking house is not so extensive."

"The newspapers have been talking about this case all week," I reminded him, "so I daresay a good number are from the press, trying to get the latest news. And then there will be the usual pack of nosy devils with nothing better to do with their time than wallow in the misfortunes of others." I walked over to the door that separated the antechamber from the courtroom, and pushed it open slightly so that the banker could hear the hubbub, amplified by the wood panelling. "Here, come and have a quick look if you like."

Fauntleroy went pale and seemed to shrink behind the curtain. "Oh no, I couldn't. But please, constable, tell me what you see."

That day there were four magistrates on the bench, the senior being Mr Conant. Then there was Sir George Farrant – a face like a fat baby, I always thought, but sharp as a tack. The other two were Mr Henry Dyer, and Mr Frederick Roe – the youngest magistrate in London at the time. Appointed only a couple of years, but we all knew he would end up running the show. The noise in the court was growing, and I feared that Mr Conant wouldn't stand for it – and indeed just then he rapped on the bench with his knuckles.

"Ladies and gentlemen," he said with obvious irritation in his voice, "this is a court of law, convened to undertake the serious business of the law. It is not a bear pit at the Vauxhall Gardens. And you are not merely disorderly but also too numerous. Some of you will need to leave the room in order that the lawyers and essential witnesses may be seated." And he gestured wearily to the chief clerk.

I closed the door.

"And now?" asked Fauntleroy.

"And now we wait," I replied.

Twenty minutes later there was a knock at the door
and the chief clerk put his head round it. "Ready," he said.
I stood by the door and indicated to Fauntleroy and
then Wilson to follow me. Mr Conant was giving a
warning to what he called sarcastically the gentlemen of
the press. "Today you may hear of some circumstances
which, if prematurely published, could impede public justice. This is an initial examination only – not a trial. If
such circumstances are revealed, I shall apprise you of
these, and am persuaded that you will feel keenly the pro-
priety of abstaining from giving premature publicity to
such matters. Any contravention of this request will
cause me to reconsider press access to any future examinations."

If the magistrate had thought to appeal to the better
nature of the newspapermen present, he failed. All he did
was alert them to the possibility of hearing something
scandalous. Vultures, they are – vultures and jackals feeding on the carcasses of other people's reputations.

As we entered the court, the crowd turned as one to
see the man of whom they had read and heard so much in
the preceding week. In the general silence that had fallen,
one woman remarked quite audibly to her companion,
"Well, he looks a deal older than forty – fifty at least, I
should have guessed!" When we reached the bar, Fauntleroy sat on the hard wooden chair provided and then

leaned forward and braced himself against the bar with his left arm, his hat held tightly in his right hand.

Four depositions that had already been given at private examinations were read out by the chief clerk, and the magistrates followed the text in the copies laid before them on the bench.

In the first, William Price, a clerk at Fauntleroy's banking house, claimed that his signature on a document had been amended by the prisoner. I saw Fauntleroy close his eyes at this last word: it was perhaps the first time that this son, brother, husband and banker had heard himself thus described. The document in question was a power of attorney, dated the seventh of December 1820, for the transfer of £10,000 of imperial three percent annuities. The shares had been held in trust for the widow of Francis William Bellis, and the trustees were Henry Fauntleroy, John Hume of the Custom House, and the surgeon John Goodchild. According to the power of attorney, the witnesses to the transfer had been James Tyson and William Price, both clerks in the house of Marsh and Company, but Price said in his deposition that although the signature was his, the words "in the presence of H Fauntleroy and J D Hume" had been added in what he believed to be Fauntleroy's handwriting. As far as Price could remember, he had signed in the presence of Fauntleroy only; Hume had not been there. Once the whole deposition had been read aloud, the chief clerk took it to William Price, who was sitting near the front of the court and making every effort not to look at Fauntleroy. Price stared at the paper before him, and signed it with a trembling hand.

In the second deposition, the Reverend Charles Hardinge, vicar of Tunbridge in Kent, gave evidence regarding another power of attorney: the signature on the document was not his, and apparently had been witnessed by a servant named John Mason, although Hardinge said he had never employed a man of that name.

The third deposition was that of John Hume – one of Fauntleroy's co-trustees for the estate of the late Francis Bellis. Hume said that his signatures on the transfers already mentioned had been forged. He also testified that, in a conversation he had had with Fauntleroy a few weeks before his arrest, the banker had assured him that all of the stock that he, Hume and Goodchild were holding in trust for the widow and children of Mr Bellis was still sitting in their joint names in the Bank of England.

The fourth deposition was that of John Goodchild. He plainly took no pleasure in giving his evidence, and for both pallor and despair his appearance could rival even that of Fauntleroy. Goodchild testified that he was a surgeon and resided at Elm Tree Row in Regent's Park, and he agreed that everything Hume and the others had said was correct. He signed his deposition and immediately left the courtroom.

One of the pack of lawyers ranged in front of the bench stood up. I recognised him as James Freshfield, who routinely represented the interests of the Bank of England. He was a tall, elegant man, the senior partner at his own firm of solicitors, and obviously at ease in this environment. From his swept-back hair, prominent nose and rather feminine mouth, you might have guessed him to be an artist rather than a lawyer. And I neither liked nor trusted him. Freshfield gathered the papers on the desk in front of him into a neat pile before saying with smooth satisfaction, "I am prepared to proceed on the earliest possible day with the charges against Mr Fauntleroy."

James Harmer now stood to represent Fauntleroy. The son of a Spitalfields weaver, Harmer had risen by dint of a good brain and hard work to his current position as one of the most respected lawyers in London. His appearance suggested a fondness for rich food and fine wine, but the excess flesh did not hide the kindliness of his eyes, and his love of high living did not prevent him from taking on seemingly hopeless cases defending those who had no means to pay for his brilliance. He was an immense man, with an immense reputation, and I both liked and trusted him. "As am I," he said to Mr Freshfield, bowing slightly.

Conant looked across at the prisoner. "I believe, Mr Fauntleroy, that you wish to remain where you are?"

"If you please, sir," Fauntleroy replied. Not that the banker had much choice: Coldbath, uncomfortable though it surely was, at least was familiar, and doubtless Harmer had explained to his client that the only alternative was Newgate.

The clerk walked to the bench and handed up a sheet of paper to Conant. The magistrate glanced at it and then addressed the banker again. "Henry Fauntleroy, you are to return to the house of correction at Coldbath Fields, to be held in custody there until your next hearing at this court on the nineteenth of October. You may go with the constable."

# CHAPTER SEVEN

# Mrs Bang

## MONDAY 20TH SEPTEMBER 1824

The rain tattooed onto the windows and I shivered as I contemplated heading out into it, wrapping my hands around my beaker of tea. We didn't know it then, but the autumn of that year would turn out to be one of the wettest ever known, and most of my memories of this case are associated with foul weather. Just as I drained my drink, Wilson put his head around the door.

"You might like to see this, sir – woman brought in for prostitution, but reckons she knows something about Mr Fauntleroy. Says she recognised him from the papers."

A fondness for paid favours could explain Fauntleroy's need for money. Men of his class rarely realised that harlots would make their money twice over: in the traditional fashion for a time, and then by blackmail for ever after. I followed Wilson to a small windowless office that we used for interviews, and instructed him to take careful notes of whatever was said; I had a feeling that we might need them. Another constable was waiting with the woman; I nodded at him and he left. I sat down opposite her and saw then that she was no more than fourteen, with thick face-paint struggling to cover the grime, and big, starved eyes trying to look bold. What she needed was a good meal and a good hiding, in that order.

"Now, Miss...?" I began.

"Angelique de la France," she said, starting to flutter her eyelashes at me and then thinking better of it. I shook my head and waited. "Angie Webster, then," she said, smiling impishly like the child she was, caught out in a fib. "Although I don't see as it's any of your business, unless you're looking for a good time." Her face suddenly fell as she realised what she had said. "Oh lor – please don't lock me up, sir – I didn't mean it!"

"I'm not going to lock you up, Angie – in fact, I might even be able to help you. Now, when you came in to the police office –"

"When I was dragged in, more like," she said primly, daintily adjusting a filthy glove.

"When you arrived here, you saw our office-keeper's newspaper on his desk and said that you recognised the man shown on the front. Is that right? This man?" I held up the paper, with the sketch of Fauntleroy on it. Done at the hearing two days earlier, it showed Fauntleroy in his blue coat and trousers, slightly stooped, clutching his hat in one hand and his gloves in the other. The face, albeit in profile, was clearly rendered.

She nodded. "I knew him straight away. That's Henry, that is." Wilson scribbled in his notebook.

"You're certain, are you?" I asked. She nodded. "And how do you know Henry? Is he a punter?"

"A punter of mine? A gent like that? Oh no: he used to come calling on a lady I worked for, as a maid."

"And why do you no longer work for her?"

"She said I stole, but I never. Men was always giving her things – jewels, gloves, hats – and sometimes she forgot where she put them. One day she said she couldn't find a bracelet, and that I took it, and so she gave me the heave-ho, the old cat."

"And Henry, was he one of the men who gave her things?"

"Oh yes, he was mad on her. I reckon he thought he was in love with her, and that she loved him back. When he started talking all serious about her settling with just him, well, she had to get rid of him."

"Didn't she want that? I would have thought he was quite a catch for her."

"Not for Mrs Bertram, no – she had bigger fish to fry than Henry. Besides, he was married; he never said at the beginning, of course, but she always had her gentlemen checked out – by one of your lot, I think – so she knew what to expect. And she was right to get rid of him, wasn't she?" She tapped her finger on the newspaper. "Look at all the trouble he's in now."

I honoured my promise to make sure that Angie wasn't charged with anything, and once we had sent her on her way with a hot drink inside her I turned to Wilson. "Good work, lad: you did well to pick up on her comment about Fauntleroy. By the way, did you recognise the name of little Angie's former employer?" I asked. He flipped back through his notes and shook his head. "Well, you have a treat in store. Let me take you to meet Mrs Bertram, but you'll need to keep your wits about you. A young man like you could easily have his head – and more – turned by our Mrs Bang."

After a quick stop at a bawdy house where the lady abbess owed me many favours and was always happy to share information about where those of her profession could be located, we set off for one of the smarter addresses in Whitehall, where Mary Bertram was living thanks to the generosity of her current patron. There, our knock was answered by a young girl in a frilly white cap and apron – Angie's successor, almost certainly.

"Is your mistress at home?" I asked.

"To both of you?" the girl asked hesitantly, peering past me at Wilson.

"We are police officers, girl, not paying visitors – now quickly, before we're soaked to the skin."

We were shown into the parlour. Wilson – taller than me, and broader too – tried to find somewhere in this most feminine of environments where he could stand or sit in comfort. Just as he had perched on a chair, our hostess came in and he leapt to his feet again. I had seen Mary Bertram a few times before, and others like her on many occasions, so I knew what to expect, and I daresay my more mature years helped too. Wilson, on the other hand, well, I suppose I threw him to the lions. He gaped and blushed, and when Mary turned to him and curtseyed prettily, he dropped his hat in confusion. No doubt used to having such an effect on men, she simply addressed me instead,

"Marguerite tells that you are police officers. How intriguing! Are you looking for a murderer, perhaps, or a highwayman?"

She waved a hand and we sat. Her large dark eyes contemplated me, their deep colour accentuated by her pale skin and fair curls. She wore a light blue dress (I made sure to remember the colour, as Martha would want to know), with a darker blue shawl over her shoulders. I couldn't help glancing down to see whether she was wearing her famous striped stockings – and indeed she was. Poor Wilson had spotted them too, and was trying to distract himself by opening his notebook.

"Not a murderer, no, ma'am," I replied. "But we are making enquiries into a gentleman who is of interest to the court, and I understand that you may be able to help us."

"Well, as you can imagine, my friends place great store by my discretion..."

"The gentleman in question is Mr Henry Fauntleroy."

"Ah – such sad times for him. But I have not seen Henry for, oh, more than a year now, so I cannot imagine that I would be of much help to you." She smiled sweetly.

"If I may explain," I said carefully. "What Constable Wilson and I are trying to ascertain is not what Mr Fauntleroy did, but rather, why he did it. It seems that he is not denying that he stole money from his customers, but so far he has offered no explanation as to why he might need to do that. And when I heard that you and he were acquainted..."

Mary Bertram laughed – a quite natural laugh, entirely at odds with the artifice of her dress and surroundings. "As a man of the world, constable, you will know that my affection does not come cheap!" Wilson stared fixedly at his notebook. "But I think I can put your mind at rest. Yes, Henry and I were lovers, but not for long. We met in Old Bond Street – I was caught in a downpour and he kindly procured me a hackney – and he started calling on me. He was certainly keen, but soon started exhibiting two characteristics that I cannot abide in a man: cheapness, and guilt. A few jewels here and there, once a fine cloak, but not enough to keep my interest. And you would think, with access to all that money..." She raised her eyebrows in amusement. "But I could have put up with that, if it hadn't been for the guilt. Always talking about what his mother would say, and what the others from his church would think – and towards the end mentioning his wife, even in bed. That's just plain rude."

I managed not to smile. "I am surprised to hear that he was so concerned about his wife; as I understood it, they led separate lives."

"Heavens, no – he doted on her, her and those two little girls. Full of ardour for me when he arrived, and the moment he was done, checking his watch and desperate to get back to Lambeth. He was fanatical about keeping our alliance secret, and at first I went along with it. But I am not made for the quiet life, gentlemen, for hiding away in a corner! It is amusing to attend balls alone once in a while, to see the sour faces of the wrinkled beldames as they flutter their fans and faint from shock, but I need a man who is willing to stand up with me in public. That wasn't Henry, so I let it be known that I was looking for a replacement. And along came dear old... well, that is another story."

"How did Mr Fauntleroy react when you told him he was no longer needed?"

She thought for a moment. "He was surprised, I think – perhaps he had been telling the truth when he said that I was his first paramour. A more experienced man would have taken it in his stride."

"Was he angry? Violent?"

"Oh no, none of that – but he wept a little, and begged me to reconsider. I had on a pearl necklace given to me by my new friend and Henry made a half-hearted attempt to snatch it from my throat. But he is not a physical man, not really, and eventually he understood that I would not change my mind. He left, and I have not seen him alone again since then. So if you are thinking, constable, that I am sitting on the fortune missing from his bank, you are mistaken!"

"Did Mr Fauntleroy ever write you any letters, arranging meetings or declaring his feelings?"

"You mean am I blackmailing him?" She shook her head. "No, Henry was particularly careful in that regard; he never communicated with me in writing. Not even a little note delivered with a gift. His training as a banker, perhaps: sweet spoken words are one thing, but write it down, in black and white, well, then you are a hostage to fortune, are you not?" She gestured at Wilson, filling his notebook.

"Indeed you are," I agreed as I stood. "You have been most helpful, Mrs Bertram."

As we walked back to Great Marlborough Street, Wilson shook his head as though to clear it. "So that's Mrs Bertram!" he said almost to himself.

I laughed; I remember that my first encounter with one of the grandes horizontales had much the same effect on me. "Also known as Mrs Bang," I commented, "in recognition of her being the most bang up to date of the ladybirds. Do you know how she started out?" Wilson said that he did not. "Well, she was born in Brighton, where her mother was a bathing-machine attendant and her father – or the man her mother says was the father – was a fisherman. Men liked the look of young Mary from an early age, and at thirteen she was seduced by a boatman. He refused to marry her, and she was ruined. The story she tells is that she was sitting in a tea room in Meeting House Lane in Brighton, sobbing quietly in genteel distress at her poor prospects, when a distinguished gentleman approached and offered her his handkerchief. He told her that he had a daughter her age in need of a companion, and that she could come to live with them in London."

"The gentleman?"

"The Earl of Barrymore – the one who limped. There was no daughter, of course, but he introduced our young Mary to a way of life that has kept her warm and dry ever since."

"Funny, isn't it," mused Wilson, "that if a poor man hires a girl out, he's a pimp, but if a titled gentleman does it, no-one thinks any the worse of him." He sighed at the injustices of our world, and then suddenly stopped and pulled his notebook from his pocket. "One thing Mrs Bertram said – yes, here it is: 'Wife and two daughters in Lambeth'. But isn't Mrs Fauntleroy down in Kent somewhere, with a son?"

I smiled; it was good to see that Wilson hadn't been completely distracted by our ladybird's charms. "I begin to think that Mr Fauntleroy is not the straightforward, hard-working, God-fearing banker he claims to be, eh, Wilson? What a man does is always infinitely less interesting than why he does it, don't you agree?"

# CHAPTER EIGHT

# The silk-merchant and the schoolgirl

## WEDNESDAY 22ND SEPTEMBER 1824

Ever since I heard him say the name with such urgency at the end of his first hearing, I had been wanting to speak to Fauntleroy's friend – or fellow banker, or whatever he might be – Freddy Lampton. Of course I did not want Fauntleroy to realise that I knew about this Lampton so I had Wilson do some quiet checking. He's a handsome lad, young Constable Wilson, and the wide-eyed maid at the banker's house certainly liked the look of him, and so we quickly learned that Freddy Lampton and Henry Fauntleroy had been friends for some years, that they often went down to Brighton together, and that Freddy could be found most days working at his uncle's silk business in Spitalfields.

The tall premises where Freddy Lampton passed his working hours was typical of the area: a small mercer's shop at the front, and weaving rooms above. How anyone in the shop could make themselves heard, or even have a sensible thought, was beyond me, with the looms clattering ceaselessly overhead. A slight, balding man of about Fauntleroy's age was leaning on some bales of fabric, totting up columns of figures in a ledger, and showing off his wares in the form of a gaudy silk waistcoat. He looked up as I walked in.

"Mr Frederick Lampton?" I asked. He nodded. "I wondered if I might ask you a few questions about Mr Henry Fauntleroy."

He quickly shut the ledger and put his head round the curtain concealing what I assumed was the living quarters at the back. "I'm going out for a while, uncle," he called. "Keep an eye on the shop, will you?" He put on his coat and hat and all but pushed me out of the door. He walked briskly down the road, with me trotting at his heels, and turned a couple of corners before coming to a churchyard. He opened the gate and indicated that I should go through and sit on a bench by the wall.

"Forgive the subterfuge," he said breathlessly, looking about him as though expecting someone to be following him. "My uncle knows nothing about Henry."

"Have you lost money in the bank?" I asked. "Did you invest your uncle's money without his knowledge and now it is gone?"

Lampton looked confused for a moment and then laughed. "Oh no, nothing like that! Henry and I meet not for business, but for pleasure. I thought that was why you wanted to talk to me."

If Lampton was not a customer of the bank, why was Fauntleroy so keen to contact him? I decided to let matters unfold themselves to me, and simply smiled encouragingly at Lampton. People will always fill a silence, I have found.

"Henry and I went to school together – well, the four of us all told, with poor William, and then John later," Lampton said after a short while. "As adults, Henry and I find the religious constraints of our families a little, let us say, irksome at times. And so we look for harmless ways to amuse ourselves."

"Visits to Brighton?" I asked, remembering what the maid had told Wilson.

He looked at me sharply. "Among other things. Billiards. Some discreet sampling of fine wines. Nothing that would trouble you and your fellow officers, constable, but all rather frowned upon by Henry's family and mine."

I nodded. "So you have no financial connection to Marsh and Company?" He shook his head. "That being so, Mr Lampton, do you have any idea why, at the end of his first appearance before the magistrate, Mr Fauntleroy was so keen that you should be informed of where he was?" Lampton hesitated. I took out my notebook and turned back through the pages. "Yes, here it is. Just before I escorted him to Coldbath, he said to Tyson – his clerk – 'Get word of my arrest to Freddy Lampton – don't forget'." I looked up at him. "Why you, Mr Lampton – of all people, why you?"

"Because I am the one who knows about Maria."

"And their two daughters?" Lampton looked at me with surprise. "Something someone else said," I explained. "But how does a man whose wife and son live in Tunbridge Wells come to have a woman and two daughters in Lambeth?"

"You can blame Brighton for that. It was four, maybe five years ago now, in the early summer. We had gone down on a Saturday morning, our usual routine, and in the late afternoon we were walking along the front towards Rottingdean when Henry met a chap he knew – George Finch. A bit of a rogue, truth be told. But with him was his sister Maria. She was a pretty little thing, sent to school in Brighton after the death of the Finch mama, and Henry fell for her straight away."

"A schoolgirl?" I asked, making notes.

"Nearly sixteen, I believe. Certainly sixteen by the time she moved to London to be with Henry."

"And what did the Finch family think of the lack of a marriage proposal?"

"George is a gambler, and his scruples were soon bought and paid for. The father died soon afterwards. And Maria, well, she decided that she would rather be with Henry on any terms than lose him. Of course their friends and neighbours in Lambeth know her as Mrs Fauntleroy – or at least they did. Some of them might have put two and two together in the past week. Poor Maria: I must go and see her again soon." He made as though to stand, but I put my hand on his arm.

"I would rather you left that to me, Mr Lampton. For the sake of those little girls, we need to think very carefully about what to do next."

# CHAPTER NINE

# The banker's key

## THURSDAY 23ᴿᴰ SEPTEMBER 1824

While I pondered how best to find out more about Maria Finch and her children, I decided that the time had come to speak to Fauntleroy's clerk Tyson. I felt that he would speak more openly away from the bank, and so I waited until I saw him leave work and followed him home. I gave him a few minutes to take off his coat and hat and kiss his wife, and then knocked. A curly-haired girl of about eight, her younger brother peeping out from behind her, opened the door and called over her shoulder to her mother. Mrs Tyson came out of the kitchen, wiping her hands on her apron, and showed me into a tiny but spotless parlour. I heard her shooing away the children and shouting up the stairs for her husband.

"Oh yes, I can remember the day I first met Henry," said James Tyson once his wife had brought us a tray of tea and closed the door behind her.

"You and Mr Fauntleroy started work at Marsh and Company at about the same time, didn't you?" I asked.

"Yes: I'd been there only about a month when his father, Mr Fauntleroy senior, brought him into the bank. Very neat and tidy, Henry was – made me look quite scruffy in comparison."

I nodded but said nothing; most people will tell you what you want to hear if you just listen instead of pushing in all the time. God gave us one mouth and two ears for a good reason, as my Martha was fond of reminding me.

"Both sixteen, we were – although of course we thought we were men about town," Tyson continued with a rueful smile. "The day he started, it was not yet time to open the doors to the public, so I was eating my breakfast in the clerks' room at the back of the bank. They caught me unawares, Henry and his father, and I nearly dropped my pie – and there I was, looking up at the most important man in the bank, with my mouth full and a kerchief tucked into my collar to protect my shirt from grease spots. I explained that Mr Robinson – chief clerk as was – had stepped out, but Mr Fauntleroy said he was looking for me. His son, he said, would be joining the bank as a clerk. Son of the managing partner, a clerk!" Tyson shook his head at the memory. "But he said that he wanted Henry to learn the business properly so that one day he too could be the managing partner. And he said that the clerks were 'the engine of the bank' – I've always remembered that. Then he asked me to show Henry around, and left us to it."

"And what did you think of the younger Mr Fauntleroy, this first time you met him?"

Tyson thought for a moment. "Well, this may sound odd, but the thing that really struck me was his hair."

"His hair?"

"Well, the cut of it, really. It was what we used to call à la Napoléon – which, at the time..."

"This was late 1810?"

"Yes, October, nearly November."

"So Mr Fauntleroy – Henry – was an admirer of the emperor?"

"And still is. He even furnished his billiard room to look like Napoleon's travelling tent, with purple silks – at least, that's what he told me it was. And his study has always had a bust of Napoleon on the mantelpiece."

"Why, do you think? Did he ever talk of it?" I asked. The newspapers had been making much of the banker's fondness for the Frenchman, using it as shorthand to suggest Fauntleroy's taste for vice and all-round untrustworthiness.

Tyson paused to consider. "I think he admires Napoleon's determination, his – what did he call it? – yes, his constancy. No matter how bleak the outlook, he often said, the Frenchman would do all he could for the cause in which he believed. Henry liked to think of himself like that, doing whatever he had to do, with the bank as his cause."

"No matter how bleak the outlook."

"Indeed," said Tyson, nodding reflectively. "Although at the beginning, of course, Henry's outlook was anything but bleak. If ever a man was born to be a banker, it was Henry. He picked up in hours the skills it took me months to master – and I soon realised that it was because he cared for his work more deeply than for anything else. I worked at Marsh and Company for the wages; he worked there because there was nowhere else he would rather be."

"So you were told to show him around. What did you tell him?" I asked as I turned to a new page in my notebook.

"I remember explaining to him what Mr Robinson had told me on my first day: the importance of routines."

I raised my eyebrows encouragingly, and waited.

"Well," Tyson elaborated, "a merchant might decide to vary his range of stock according to fashion. A lawyer might, perhaps, close his office early to take advantage of a sunny summer's day. But a banker must be predictable and reliable: the bank must be open at the same time on the same days, it must complete its ledgers in the same way for every transaction, it must act precisely and promptly against every instruction, or trust will be lost. And a bank that has lost the trust of its customers has lost everything."

We both sat silently for a moment as the import of what Tyson had just said settled upon us.

"Anyway," he continued, "Henry followed me everywhere for the first few days, always with a notebook in his hand – one a bit like yours. Always jotting down something. And always questioning. One day, for instance, I showed him the signature cards – you've seen those in banks before?"

I nodded. "You mean the little cards, in a large wooden tray?"

"Exactly. So I took one out to show Henry, putting a stick in the tray to mark my place, just as Mr Robinson had taught me. Henry studied the card carefully; like all the others, it had on it a clearly written name, a signature, a date and then another signature – that of his father, Mr Fauntleroy senior. I explained that the signature cards are completed in front of us on the day the customer joins the bank, and that only a partner or the senior clerk can witness them – not ordinary clerks, as we were then. So it's proof of the customer's signature. Then whenever we receive an instruction from a customer, before we do anything with it, we check the signature on the instruction against the signature card."

"To make sure that it's really from that customer, and not from someone else signing their name?"

Tyson nodded. "Funny: that's exactly the same question as Henry asked me back then. At the time, I couldn't really see what use that would be to anyone – why would you want to move someone else's money around, I wondered? I'm older and wiser now."

"Is there anything else you remember about your first impressions of Mr Fauntleroy?"

"I remember commenting on his neat writing; mine has always been a scrawl, and they do like clear writing in banks. I asked whether they had taught him his penmanship at his fancy school, and he didn't like that at all. I didn't know then about the difficulties the Fauntleroys had, with their beliefs."

"Difficulties?"

"Henry said that he and his brothers – you know about his older brother William?"

"I know something of him. I should like to know more."

"I doubt Henry will tell you much – he rarely talks of it." Tyson drained his cup and put it back on the tray. "But it changed him, when William died – of that I have no doubt." He looked away.

I waited a few seconds and suspected that he had forgotten what we were discussing. "You were talking of difficulties," I prompted him. "With their beliefs."

"Ah yes. Well, the three boys (there's a younger brother John as well) had wanted to go to grammar school, Henry said, but with them being Dissenters, they weren't allowed to. The school wouldn't have them. So they went to, what was it he called it, an academy instead – for people like them. Henry said that it was just like a grammar school, the same disciplines – a big long list of them – French, Italian, history – made my head ache just thinking of it all. So I said that with all of that he could have gone to university. But Dissenters can't go to university in England, he said – did you know that?"

I shook my head.

"No, nor me. Scotland, perhaps, or Holland, apparently, but not here. But it made no difference to Henry anyway. He said he wasn't interested in being a lawyer or a school-teacher – all he ever wanted to be was a banker."

"And you?" I asked.

Tyson looked surprised. "Me? No, for me it was just an escape. My dad was a porter at Smithfield – dirty, back-breaking work that killed him too young – not for me, thanks very much."

The son of a lighterman myself, I understood only too well. "So you and Mr Fauntleroy settled into life as clerks at the bank. Did he do or say anything back then that you particularly remember? Anything that made you uneasy?"

Tyson frowned slightly as he thought back – after all, it was nearly fifteen years ago. "Well, I suppose the thing that troubles me sometimes is the key."

"The key," I echoed, turning to another new page in my notebook.

"The key to the main doors of the bank," he explained. "As managing partner, Henry's father had one, of course, and so did Mr Robinson, as chief clerk. But everyone knew that there was a third key, that would be given to a junior clerk only once he had proved himself to be eminently reliable and honest."

"Why give such responsibility to a junior clerk?"

"It was Mr Robinson's idea. He was getting on a bit, and on cold, dark mornings when Mr Fauntleroy senior was off elsewhere, he didn't like having to make an early start to open up the bank. And he thought that having a key would teach a junior clerk care, and loyalty. It was nearly a year since Henry and I had started at the bank, and all the juniors knew that Mr Robinson was about to announce who the third key would be given to, and moreover we all knew that only we two were in the running. Late one afternoon, I was tidying my area of the bench in preparation for going home when Henry came up to me and asked if I had time for a quick drink. Knowing that he didn't like to drink close to home, in case one of his father's Dissenter friends saw him, I suggested a place in Holborn.

"The keeper brought our beer, and I waited for Henry to say what was on his mind. It seemed to take him an age to get his thoughts in order, but finally he came out with it. 'About this key business,' he said. 'We both know that whoever is asked to keep the key will also be given some extra money. To compensate for the responsibility.' It was three shillings a week, which I sorely needed at the time. My younger brothers were growing like weeds, and my sister Sally was about to start courting – and I quite fancied the idea of being able to take a wife myself, so I'd need something to offer her. I hadn't said all of that to Henry, but he knew. His next question made that clear. 'Is it the key itself you want?' he asked. 'Do you want the trust and responsibility – or is it really the extra money?' No-one likes to admit they need money, though, do they, so I kept quiet and drank my beer.

"And then he came out with it. 'Listen, Jim,' he said. 'I'm not bothered about the money – I don't have your outgoings. But I need to start making my own way at the bank. I know I got my position because of my father.' I thought about denying it, but we both knew it was true. 'That said, I'm a good clerk, and I don't think Marsh and Company is any the poorer for having me there. But I need to start proving my own worth, to show that I'm a fine banker in my own right, and not just the son of William Fauntleroy.' Well, I had to laugh at his ambition – here he was, not even a chief clerk yet, and talking about being a banker in his own right. He didn't laugh, though; instead he reached across the table and grasped my wrist. 'You'll see: one day I'll be the best-known banker in all London,' he said. And he was right, wasn't he?" Tyson laughed sadly. "The best-known banker in all London."

"What happened with the key?" I asked, although I had already guessed.

"Well, Henry came up with a solution to suit us both," answered Tyson. "I told Mr Robinson that, with my family obligations, I couldn't get to the bank early enough, and so he gave the key to Henry – he was never going to be late, living just next door. And Henry passed the three shillings a week on to me."

A very neat solution, I thought: for Fauntleroy to have unfettered and undisturbed access to the bank whenever he wanted would be worth every penny of three shillings a week to him.

# CHAPTER TEN

# A Saturday in Vauxhall

## SATURDAY 25TH SEPTEMBER 1824

Two birds with one stone, I congratulated myself. Martha often complained that I rarely took her out, and I wanted to see for myself this young woman who lived as Henry Fauntleroy's wife, and so that Saturday I suggested to Martha that we treat ourselves to a day in the gardens at Vauxhall. We started out early, as it is a fair walk from home, but thankfully the weather was fine and we always enjoyed each other's company.

I had Fauntleroy's address from his friend Lampton, and under the pretext of needing some refreshment, I persuaded Martha to take a drink in the Robin Hood public house on South Lambeth Road – which just happened to be opposite Fauntleroy's house, the last in a row of four neat houses set back from the road.

As I was looking across at them, the front door to number 4 Lawn Villas opened and out came a slight young woman with masses of dark curly hair caught up inexpertly under a bonnet. She manoeuvred a perambulator out into the street, and then indicated to the little girl following her to hold onto her skirt. They walked down the road towards the gardens and disappeared from sight. I turned back to my drink and found Martha watching me levelly.

"And who was that?" she asked. There was no point lying – she always knows when I am.

"Maria Finch," I said. "And those are her children – hers and Henry Fauntleroy's."

"I see," said Martha, with the tiny beginnings of a smile. "And do you expect me to believe that this is the most enormous coincidence? That we should go on our annual outing together and just happen to see the family of the man you are currently investigating?"

I hung my head in mock shame. Martha drained her glass.

"Well," she said, standing and gathering her things, "we'd better look sharp if we're going to catch up with them."

We left the public house and hurried across the road, turning the same corner as Miss Finch, and were just in time to see her going through the entrance gate into Vauxhall Gardens. I started to quicken my pace, but Martha took hold of my arm.

"Let me. You'll only alarm her. You wait near the entrance, and I'll come and find you."

Just inside the gate I sat on a bench and watched a nursemaid trying to control two boisterous lads while smiling over her shoulder at a guardsman. It was one of the rare warm days we had that September, and I ran a finger round the inside of my collar to loosen it. I fully intended simply to rest for a moment, but the sounds of children's laughter, the sun playing through the trees and the pint of beer soon over-powered me and I nodded off.

By the time Martha returned and shook me awake, the nursemaid and the guardsman had both gone – although whether together or separately, I could not say. Martha sat down next to me and fanned her hand in front of her face.

"Well?"

"Well you might ask," she said with some vigour. "Left her to struggle alone, hasn't he – her and those two little mites. Elizabeth is just three, and Charlotte still a babe in arms." She shook her head. "How are they going to manage without a father?"

I took her hand. "Plenty do, my love."

"Aye, but it doesn't make it right, does it?" She sniffed and blinked away a tear. "Anyway, it's as you said. They met in Brighton and he brought her to London. He never promised marriage, she said – he already had a wife, he told her, but didn't live with her as a husband."

"Did he tell her why?"

Martha nodded. "He said that there was a baby, but that the baby died, and his wife couldn't bear to look at him after that."

"I suppose he didn't want her to know that he is the sort of man who can abandon his child. Better to say that the boy died, than have to explain why he never sees him."

"She said that he's a wonderful father to her two, always petting and spoiling them."

"But still not giving them his name, or any security when he's gone. Did she tell you anything more about him?"

Martha shook her head. "Not much. She didn't even tell me his full name – just called him 'my Henry'. Lonely, I think she is, poor girl – that's why she was so chatty with me, I should imagine. Anyway, when I asked where her Henry was on such a lovely day, she said that he was in prison, but that it was just a silly mistake and that people would soon realise that he had already put it all right and then he would be freed."

"So she knows all about the forgery. I daresay Lampton told her."

Martha shook her head. "No: I got the impression that she knew even before the arrest. She said something about him telling her about irregular dealings at his bank, long before he knew her, and that he had put it all straight but people haven't realised yet."

"So here she is, expecting him to come home at any minute, while we know that he is facing the – well, the worst. What sort of a man lies to the mother of his children like that?"

Martha squeezed my hand. "Plenty of bad men have children, Sam, and plenty of good ones don't." She sighed and straightened her hat. "Come on: let's get home. There's a nice piece of ham waiting for us."

# CHAPTER ELEVEN

# The elder brother

## MONDAY 27ᵀᴴ SEPTEMBER 1824

"It's a cruel disease, that's for sure," said Martha as she cleared the plates from the table a couple of evenings later. "I pity anyone having to watch a loved one die from that." She shook her head in sympathy, soft-hearted as ever. "Only twenty-two, you say? A young man, with everything ahead of him."

In my years as a police officer, I have seen sights and heard tales that would make a brave man hide his face, and I have worked steadily on. What none of my fellow constables knows is that at the end of a harrowing day I come home to Martha and pour it all out to her, sometimes ending by sobbing in her arms like the child we both wished for but no longer discussed. That evening I wasn't crying, but I couldn't face my bed without telling her what I had heard, and hearing in turn her gently comforting murmurs as she sat by the fire and tended to her mending.

As soon as I had arrived at Great Marlborough Street that morning, I had been accosted by Nate Simpson, one of the court clerks.

"You've been dealing with Fauntleroy, forgery, right?" he said, flipping through the sheaf of papers in his hand. He looked up at me expectantly and I nodded. "Mr Conant wants to see you."

My blood ran cold: had Fauntleroy done himself some harm, as the magistrate had feared? I made my way quickly up to Mr Conant's dining room, but his own relaxed demeanour reassured me; he simply indicated that I should wait for a moment while he finished his breakfast. He drained his cup and wiped his mouth with a napkin, then leaned back in his chair.

"So, constable," he asked, "how are your enquiries progressing?"

"I would have written you a report, sir," I explained, "but I thought that it might be more secure to tell you in person – I was planning to visit Mr Fauntleroy later this week." The magistrate nodded and I continued. "I've been looking into his personal circumstances – rather more complicated than they might initially appear. A wife and a mistress."

Conant shook his head ruefully. "That can be an expensive business," he mused. "Did you manage to speak to that tall clerk of his?"

"James Tyson, yes," I replied. "I don't think he's involved, sir – seemed like a square fellow to me."

The magistrate steepled his hands and looked across them at me. "Well, Mr Fauntleroy's due before me again in, what, three weeks' time. Find out what you can, there's a good man. Go and see him sooner rather than later, I think – after sitting in that ghastly place for a fortnight, he'll be glad to see a friendly face and might be a bit more forthcoming."

No time like the present, and so as soon as I had left Mr Conant's apartment I jumped into a hackney and set off for Coldbath Fields. A turnkey led me through the familiar corridors to Fauntleroy's cell and – as the magistrate had foreseen – the banker rose to his feet, a smile on his face and his hand outstretched in welcome.

"Constable Plank," he said, with warmth in his voice. "What a pleasure to see you. Two visitors in one morning – I am certainly spoilt. Did you pass Mr Hanson on your way in?"

"No, sir," I said. I was surprised: apart from family members and his lawyer, Fauntleroy was not permitted visitors. Fauntleroy indicated one of the two rickety chairs and I sat down, balancing my notepad on my knee. "Can you describe this Mr Hanson?" I asked.

"Elderly," said the banker. "And respectable-looking. He had a black book in his hand – a Bible as it turned out. I stood up to greet him when the turnkey let him in, and he asked whether I was the banker from Berners Street, and I said that I was. Then he said that I had better look to my soul and look to my Bible, that I should read my Bible. He waved his black book at me, and left as suddenly as he had arrived."

"Did the turnkeys say anything?" I asked.

"Newcombe put his head round the door soon after-wards, and so I asked him who the man was. He told me that it was John Hanson the magistrate, and that he had said that he knew me."

That made some sense: magistrates are permitted to demand access to any house of correction and any pris-oner within it. "And do you know him, sir?" I asked.

"No: I've never heard of him, and never seen him be-fore today."

I made a few more notes. "Mr Conant will want to know about this; I'll pass on what you have told me." And then, as the banker seemed to be in an expansive mood, I decided to take a chance. "As I'm here, sir, I wondered if I might talk to you about something else, something that someone hinted might be important to your case."

"Of course, constable," said Fauntleroy pleasantly. "It is not as though I have other appointments pressing on my time today. How can I be of help?"

"Well, sir, I wanted to talk to you about your brother."

"John? Yes, he is helping Mr Harmer with my defence, but he's not really a criminal lawyer..." He trailed off as he saw me shaking my head.

"Not that brother, sir. I wanted to ask you about William Fauntleroy."

The smile faded from the banker's face, and he gripped the edge of the table with one hand. "But William – he died over twenty years ago. How can he be of relevance to my present situation, constable?"

I wondered then just how honest Mr Harmer had been with his client about that present situation. Did Fauntleroy know that he faced the noose, or did he imagine that the law would operate differently for someone with his education and connections?

"At your trial," I explained, "the judge will want to know why you did what you are accused of doing. It is the duty of your lawyer to explain what has driven you to this, and it has been suggested to me that the death of your brother may form part of that explanation. Mr Conant thought that it might be helpful to your defence if you were to consider anything that could be put in mitigation for you." There. I had asked. There was no other

way to put it, and so I waited. The skill to seeking information is knowing when to stop asking for it.

"I was nineteen years old," began Fauntleroy in a voice
that sounded as though it was coming from the bottom of
a well. "The coughing seemed never to end – on and on
it went, for weeks. The night William died I had been
sitting as usual on the edge of his bed, in my nightshirt,
patting him hard on the back as the doctor had shown me.
I despaired to feel the boniness of my brother's frame, the
way I was able to support its wasted weight so easily, but
I made sure not to let him see my concern. Our parents
had appointed a nurse to see to William's needs during
the day, but at night, during the terrible bouts of coughing and sweating, I cared for him in our shared room. I
think it suited both of us. William was used to an active
and energetic life, and being confined to bed as an invalid
made him irritable and sulky with the nurse. And after a
day of impersonal efficiency at the bank, I welcomed the
opportunity for human contact. And of course we both
knew enough about consumption to realise that our time
together was very precious."

Fauntleroy's voice caught slightly, and I waited for
him to continue.

"Anyway, Will was feeling philosophical that night,
and as I wiped the blood from his chin and handed him a
glass of water, he asked me, 'Where do you think we go

next, Henry?' I tried to make light of it, telling him that I was off to the Bank of England in the morning, but he was serious. 'You know what I mean,' he said. 'When we die.' I shifted so that I was sitting up against a pillow with my arm around Will's shoulder and his head resting on my chest. He had always been taller than me, but the illness had diminished him so much.

"I tried to give him an answer that would comfort him. 'Well, you believe in Jesus Christ, don't you?' I said. 'And you've lived a good life, and prayed for the forgiveness of your sins?' He nodded. 'Then the Bible says that you shall go to Heaven and enjoy life everlasting.' But Will was never one to accept something so simplistic. 'But what if Paine is right, Henry, and the Bible cannot be relied upon? What then?' Of course I had no answer for that: Will was the reader and thinker in the family. Numbers are all I have ever understood. 'How am I to manage when you are gone, Will?' I asked. 'Who will tell me what to read and what to believe?'

"He had obviously anticipated this, because he gestured weakly to his overflowing bookcases, with even more volumes stacked up against them on the floor, and several open on the table with slips of paper marking important passages. 'There, Henry – you can start with those. I am happy to leave you my books, as I know you will cherish them. But I beg of you: do not touch my paints and brushes! You may know the value of a piece of art as an asset or a commodity, but you do not know the first thing about creating one. The paints and brushes are to go to Lizzie, who will treat them with the delicacy they deserve. But there are two sketches I wish you to have; the rest will go to Mama and Papa, but two are for you. They're in that green portfolio leaning against the wardrobe – bring them to me.'

"I fetched the portfolio. William untied the laces, and took out two unframed drawings, each about a foot square. The first was of the Thames during a Frost Fair – the very first Frost Fair that we had attended together as boys. 1795, I think it was. There were the makeshift stalls, the animals with clouds of breath steaming from their nostrils, the crowds of people clinging to each other and laughing as they tried to stay upright on the unfamiliar ice. We both smiled as we looked at the picture together, remembering the adventure and excitement of that day. The second drawing was of me, done just a few months previously at a picnic in Hyde Park. I hadn't realised that Will was sketching me, and he chuckled weakly. 'Yes – you were too busy looking at the girls in their summer dresses to notice what I was up to. I think it's rather like, don't you?'

"And he was right: it was very like. The expert pencil lines had caught my features exactly: there were my high forehead and long nose, my prominent chin and angular cheekbones." Fauntleroy held his head at an angle to demonstrate. "But what I really wanted was a portrait of William. I asked if he had one, and he shook his head. 'A self-portrait? What kind of artist spends his time looking at himself when there's the rest of the world to see? You'll have to remember me for yourself, Henry: take a good look while I doze for a while.'" The banker seemed not to notice the tears on his cheeks. "It was the last thing he said to me."

Martha dabbed at her eyes with the corner of her apron. "That poor man," she said, shaking her head. "No-one should see a brother suffer like that." And I knew that she was thinking of little George and later Albert, both barely out of swaddling before she and her parents had had to bid them farewell. "And the burial – Bunhill Fields?"

I nodded. "His mother and father were there, of course, and his sister – but from all accounts the father was of little use."

"Stunned by his own grief, more than likely."

"Aye – and so Fauntleroy had to be the strength of the family for the women. Funny the thing he told me he remembered, after all these years. He said that the minister's cassock was ill-fitting and short, showing his boots, which he had neglected to polish. Showed a lack of respect, Fauntleroy said. And then he gave me, well, an obituary of sorts, I suppose. I promised to return it to him when we next meet – it seemed very dear to him." I passed the page to her, torn from *The Gentleman's Magazine* and dated the first of November 1803.

Martha read it to herself and then looked up at me. "Well, they seemed to rate this William Fauntleroy very highly, didn't they? Amiable young man, they call him – with an active mind, often making brilliant remarks. Seems he had it all at his feet. Losing a brother like that would quite shake your faith in the goodness of the world." She sighed and pushed herself up from her chair, handing William's obituary back to me.

"And make you determined to seize every opportunity in your own life?" I suggested. "To take chances, in case they never come up again?"

Martha nodded. "It's just as you always say, Sam: you need only look into a man's past to see his future."

# CHAPTER TWELVE

# The power of attorney

TUESDAY 19TH OCTOBER 1824

As it turns out, it was fully three weeks before I saw Fauntleroy again and could return his brother's obituary to him. On the morning of his third appearance before the magistrates, I returned to Coldbath Fields. I could have sent another officer, but I wanted more time alone with the banker. Once he was in the courtroom he would withdraw into himself, but on the short journey from Coldbath, well, he might say something. As always, he was courtesy itself as I led him to the hackney waiting for us at the gates.

"Are you well, constable?" he asked.

I nodded. "Stout as an oak, as my mother always said, thank you, sir," I answered. "Wooden by name, wooden

by nature. But you're a little pale sir, if you don't mind
my saying," I commented as I climbed into the hackney
behind him.

"Thank you for your concern, constable. The truth is
that I am not sleeping well – my mind races during the
hours of darkness. I understand that there is much material to present, but I do wish to heaven that two hearings
had sufficed. I am filled with dread at the thought of facing that pack again." He shrank away from the window
as he spoke.

And his fear was justified, for if anything the crowd
outside the court was even more pressing than before;
thanks to the efforts of the principal London papers,
there can have been few people in the capital who did not
know something of the case, and the majority of them had
an opinion on it. Once again I led the banker to the bar,
and once again he faced Mr Conant, Mr Farrant and Mr
Dyer on the bench. This time the chief clerk whispered
as I passed him that Cornelius Buller, the governor of the
Bank of England, and his deputy John Baker Richards
were in court. As before, their lawyer Freshfield represented them at the barristers' table, and sitting across the
table from him were James Harmer and John Forbes.
Both nodded at Fauntleroy as he took his place. I stood
beside him, disappearing as a policeman in uniform can
do so easily in a courtroom. Ask any criminal how many

policemen were in attendance at his trial, and he won't be able to tell you.

Mr Conant spoke first to Fauntleroy, who looked up in surprise; I don't think he expected to be addressed directly. "Mr Fauntleroy, I understand that a Mr Hanson called at your cell some weeks ago, and spoke to you in an unpleasant, if not insulting, tone."

Fauntleroy nodded

"Mr Hanson," continued Mr Conant with distaste evident in his voice, "is a magistrate from Hammersmith. As you doubtless know, magistrates are permitted to visit houses of correction whenever they wish, to ensure that they are up to standard, and so neither Mr Hanson nor the keeper nor turnkeys broke any rules in permitting him access to your cell. However, Mr Fauntleroy, I understand that the manner and the spirit of his visit were insulting. I am sorry that such an occurrence should have taken place, and I shall take care to prevent a repetition of it."

Fauntleroy stood, and everyone in the court leaned forward slightly to see and hear him more clearly. He was wearing the same dark, well-cut outfit as at the previous hearing, with the addition of a striped waistcoat that his brother John had brought to the gaol for him. His voice was quiet but unhesitating and measured; to my mind, it suggested a man well in control of his emotions.

"Please do not trouble, sir," he said. "Mr Hanson did nothing insulting beyond intruding into my chamber without my prior invitation."

"Nonetheless," concluded Mr Conant, "Mr Hanson has been struck off the list of visiting justices." He made a dismissive gesture with his hand. "Now to the proper business of the day. Mr Freshfield, you may begin."

Freshfield waited until all attention in court was on him before rising to his feet. "I would like to introduce evidence of two further charges against the prisoner. The first concerns a power of attorney allegedly signed by Colonel Lyster, of Wexford in Ireland. If we could bring Colonel Lyster to give evidence..."

Just like the witnesses at the first hearing, Colonel Lyster – a military man to his core and still upright in his sixties – confirmed that he had supplied a limited power of attorney to Marsh and Company, authorising them to receive dividends and pay them into his account, but that a later full power of attorney bore a signature that was not his own. Colonel Lyster quit the court, and the second witness of the day was called. When he walked into court, I could hear whispers all around me of "The uncle, the uncle!"

Jedediah Kerie was the older brother of Fauntleroy's mother Elizabeth and – like all the Fauntleroy relations, it turns out – had been a customer of the Berners Street bank. Slim and dapper like his nephew, but with the slight stoop of age, he looked straight ahead as he passed us at the bar, although I could see from the clench of his jaw that this was an effort. Once on the stand, he was handed the power of attorney that had been referred to by Colonel Lyster, but had to dab at his eyes with a handkerchief before he could examine the document. Freshfield pointed to the part that he wished Kerie to read.

"Mr Kerie, what does this document say, at the bottom, below the signature purporting to be that of Colonel Lyster?" he asked.

"It says," started Kerie, but his voice cracked with emotion. "It says," he began again, and once more a sob broke from him.

"Take your time, Mr Kerie," said Mr Conant. "The court is aware of your family connection to the defendant, and makes due allowance for it. Nevertheless, you must answer truthfully the questions put to you by Mr Freshfield."

Kerie nodded and drew himself up. Beside me, Fauntleroy seemed to be affected by the distress of his uncle, and pressed his own handkerchief to his eyes. Kerie lifted the document again and it trembled in his hand. "Below the signature, it says, 'Signed, sealed and delivered in the presence of Jedediah Kerie of Lawler Place, Bath'."

"And what then?" prompted Freshfield.

"Then there is my name."

"Not your signature?"

Kerie paused and for the first time looked directly at his nephew, who could not meet his eye. "No," he said. "It is my name, but it is not my signature. Neither the attestation nor the signature is in my writing."

"To be absolutely clear, sir," asked Freshfield, "are you saying that you did not witness Colonel Lyster signing this document?"

For some moments Kerie could not reply but simply shook his head. Eventually, through his tears, he whispered, "No, sir, I did not."

At an indication from Mr Conant, Kerie was helped from the stand and escorted from the room.

James Tyson was then brought into court. Once on the stand, he too was shown the vexed power of attorney.

"Turn your attention, if you would, Mr Tyson, to the attestation," said Freshfield. "We have already heard from Mr Kerie that the attestation is not in his handwriting. So it must have been written by someone else. Do you recognise the handwriting, Mr Tyson?"

Tyson took hold of the document and examined it carefully, turning it to catch the best light. After a long minute he replied. "Yes, sir, I believe I do."

"And whose handwriting do you think it is?"

"In my opinion, sir, it is the handwriting of Mr Henry Fauntleroy." Gasps were heard all around the courtroom.

"And you are familiar with the prisoner's handwriting, are you, Mr Tyson?"

"I am, sir, yes."

"Because you are his clerk, and you have cause to see it every day. Is that not right, Mr Tyson?"

"Yes, sir. I know his hand as well as I know my own."

Finally, wringing every last drop of drama from that wretched power of attorney, Freshfield called George Hutchinson, a clerk at the Bank of England. Nervously, in a jacket a little too long and a collar a little too loose, Hutchinson made his way across the room. When he saw his governor and deputy governor sitting together and watching him, whatever slight colour he had in his face drained away completely. He took the stand and was shown the document.

"Mr Hutchinson," said Freshfield, "have you seen this document before?"

Hutchinson swallowed hard, and his prominent Adam's apple bobbed. "Yes, sir, I have."

"On what occasion?"

"It was presented to me, sir."

"Once, Mr Hutchinson?"

"Twice, sir."

"Twice?"

"Yes, sir."

"And to what end?" prompted Freshfield.

"On – on – on each occasion it was to support a request to transfer £3,000 of stock, which I fulfilled, sir."

"£3,000 of stock on two occasions – so £6,000 of stock in all," said Freshfield. "And can you remember who presented this document to you?"

"I can, sir. It was that gentleman there." And Hutchinson pointed at Fauntleroy.

"The prisoner at the bar? Both times? Henry Fauntleroy presented this document to you on two occasions, occasioning the transfer of £6,000 of stock?"

"Yes, sir." Hutchinson caught sight of Buller, who was shaking his head sadly, and looked down at his feet.

"Thank you, Mr Hutchinson. You may leave," said Freshfield. He turned to the bench. "That is the end of my evidence regarding Colonel Lyster's document. I shall now turn my attention to long annuities."

The rest of the afternoon was spent in hearing the evidence of various clerks. After the excitement of the earlier witnesses these were rather dull fare, and several people left the room, pushing and shoving their way out. Fauntleroy slumped impassive at the bar, his head resting on his arm, and occasionally sighing. Freshfield questioned each clerk in turn, making rather a meal of it, but I suppose he was trying to demonstrate the banking process to people who were still coming to terms with the idea of value that could be represented not by gold coin but by paper money and even by stock certificates. Finally, dismissing the last of his witnesses, Freshfield bowed to the bench and sat down with an air of satisfaction.

Mr Conant gathered his papers, and those who remained in the court settled like birds onto their perches. At a nudge from Mr Harmer, John Forbes sprang to his feet.

"If it please the court," he said, "we would request that our client be permitted to return to Coldbath Fields for a further two days. This will enable us more easily to receive instructions as to how to proceed."

The magistrate looked at Forbes, and then at Fauntleroy, who sat at the bar with his shoulders hunched. The crowd waited with a collective indrawn breath.

"I see no reason to deny the request," said Mr Conant after a few moments. "The prisoner is to return to Coldbath Fields, and from there will be taken to Newgate on Thursday of this week – Thursday is the general removing day for prisoners, I believe."

At the mention of the name of Newgate, Fauntleroy groaned quietly and, before I could reach up to him, fell from his chair in a faint. As he slid to the floor, I heard a woman's voice cry out: "Someone help him, oh please someone help him!" Pushing her way through the crowd was Maria Finch, which certainly gave the vultures something to pick over in the next day's newspapers.

# CHAPTER THIRTEEN

# Bankers to the banks

## WEDNESDAY 20TH OCTOBER 1824

Seeing Buller and Richards at the hearing had given me an idea, and I acted on it the very next day. The pale stone of the Bank of England stood out dramatically against the grey autumn sky as I walked up Lothbury. Tivoli Corner, as they had started calling it, looked more like a Grecian temple than the public entrance to a bank, but then I suppose that this was where men came to worship money. Following the huge wall rearing up alongside me – fire-proof and riot-proof, according to the architect – I turned into St Bartholomew Lane and gave my name and business to the doorman guarding the bank's offices.

After waiting in an outer chamber for upwards of half an hour, as though my time were of no consequence, I

was called through to an inner room. A man sitting behind one of the largest desks I have ever seen got to his
feet with a grunt. Charles Foster was about fifty, and
dressed in a sober outfit that creaked and strained at every
seam. Good living had caused this particular banker to
the banks to swell, while spending all daylight hours in-
doors had turned his skin pale and waxy, so that the over-
all impression was that of an over-stuffed sausage. He
eased himself back into his chair, and indicated with a re-
gal wave of his chubby hand that I should take the smaller,
less commodious seat on the other side of his vast desk.

"Constable Plank," he began, "I understand that you
are here to talk about that rogue Fauntleroy."

Something in his self-satisfied tone irritated me.
"Henry Fauntleroy has been accused of a number of
frauds, yes, and I am trying to ascertain the facts behind
the accusations," I said stiffly. "Mr Fauntleroy has told his
lawyer that he came to see you some years ago about extending his bank's credit, and that you refused. He claims
that it was this refusal that was the root of his current
troubles. Do you recall that meeting?"

"We are talking about a meeting nearly a decade ago,
constable, and not even a very memorable one at that:
Fauntleroy is not the first banker to overstretch himself
and expect us to ride to his rescue. However, we do not
need to rely on my memory, as here at the Bank we keep
a careful record of all meetings." Foster pulled a leather-

covered ledger towards him and opened it at a marker. He read down the page, pursed his lips and looked up. "Ah yes, I remember him now. Small, prim – rather too fond of his tailor."

"His personal appearance is not of relevance. Or is that all that your records note?"

Foster stared at me, probably trying to work out whether I was being insolent or merely factual. He let it drop. He looked down again at his ledger and started to read.

"Wednesday the third of May 1815, eleven o'clock. Henry Fauntleroy, managing partner of Marsh and Company, asked for an extension of credit owing to 'a slight embarrassment of funds'. I have put that in quotation marks, so we know that those were his exact words."

I looked up from my notebook. "And was that an accurate description of the position of his banking house at the time?"

"It was not: their debts were much more extensive. I see here that Fauntleroy went on to claim that he had put in place a plan to 'regularise this unusual state of affairs' – again, his words. He also invoked the name of his father, perhaps hoping to convince me that he shared Mr William Fauntleroy's prudent nature, but I was not fooled. The father, now, there was a steady hand on the tiller – not a moment's bother when he was in charge."

"Did you turn down Henry Fauntleroy's request simply on the basis that he was not his father?" I asked.

"Constable Plank, the Bank of England is not in the habit of allowing personal views to influence professional decisions. I am not sure that you quite grasp the gravity and importance of our role in the modern world of banking." He stood with some effort and went to gaze out of his office window into the courtyard, in the manner of a general surveying his troops. I had the impression that I was about to hear a speech, and I was right. "We are bankers to the banks; we are the foundation on which the financial world is built. I explained to Fauntleroy – as I have explained to many others like him, before and since – that we at the Bank bear a heavy responsibility. We owe a duty of care to many banks – not just here in England, but across the globe. If I had permitted Fauntleroy's bank to continue on the same path, I would have been taking a risk with other people's money – and this we are not permitted to do." He turned to face me. "I therefore refused to extend any more credit to Marsh and Company."

"What was Mr Fauntleroy's reaction?"

Foster glanced down at his ledger. "His reaction was of no consequence to me or to the Bank. There is no note of it here." He closed the ledger carefully and pushed it to the furthest edge of his desk, as though further contact with it would contaminate him with failure.

# CHAPTER FOURTEEN

# Newgate

THURSDAY 21ST OCTOBER 1824

As dusk fell on the day following my unpleasant meeting at the Bank of England, I walked into the courtyard of Coldbath Fields to accompany Henry Fauntleroy to Newgate. Waiting for me were John Vickery and the turnkey Newcombe. Other turnkeys were gathered by the gate, and Fauntleroy was shaking hands with each of them in turn. The two horses stepped on the spot, their harness jingling as they shook their heads, their breath clouding in the cooling night air. One of the turnkeys handed Fauntleroy's small trunk and writing desk up to the driver, and he strapped them onto the roof.

The banker, the keeper and I climbed into the hackney, and as we jolted off through the gathering dark Fauntleroy asked Vickery about Newgate. He affected a

casual tone but gave away his true state of mind by gnawing at the corner of a fingernail.

"There's no need to fret, sir," said Vickery in kindly
tones. "Wontner, the keeper there, is a good man, I assure
you. Used to be a marshal in the city, so he understands
the law and its processes. He's no brute, sir, not at all."

I had heard much the same, and I nodded in agreement. Many keepers had a well-earned reputation for
sadism and cruelty, and doubtless tales of their savagery
had been told and retold in Coldbath, but John Wontner
was not of their number.

"He's a peg-leg," added Vickery as an afterthought.
"Came off his horse a couple of years ago – nasty business.
That's why he left the force; a one-legged man's no use to
them."

The hackney swung round the corner into Newgate
Street and stopped alongside a short, narrow flight of
steps leading up to a door set deep into a stone archway.
As he alighted, Fauntleroy glanced upwards. The
wooden door had two rows of iron teeth along its top
edge, and across the stone arch was an elaborate carving
of swags of heavy chains. He shuddered, and I could understand why.

Just inside the door, John Wontner was waiting for us
– a kindly looking man with a compact, muscular build.
He ushered us into a dark hallway where a desk stood

with a candle burning low on it, casting dancing shadows up the walls. Once the outer door had been secured, Wontner led us into his office. A small barred window looked out into the street, and a delicate white vase stood on the window-sill with a single pale pink rose in it. Wontner caught me looking at it, and smiled apologetically.

"My wife," he said by way of explanation. "Ladies do try to make the best of any surroundings – which is one of the reasons we love them, is it not?"

Fauntleroy gave a tight smile and sat in the chair that Wontner was indicating. Vickery took a seat against the wall, while I remained standing with my back to the door. Wontner himself sat at his desk and pulled a folder towards him. "You are Henry Fauntleroy, banker of Berners Street?" he asked, reading from a sheet on top of the folder.

"I am," replied Fauntleroy.

"Born the twelfth of October in 1784?" He glanced up, and the banker nodded. "Then I have the senior of you by six months, Mr Fauntleroy, for I was born in February of the same year. Now I have here your commitment, Mr Fauntleroy, which was delivered to me this morning. Please listen carefully. 'Receive into your custody the body of Henry Fauntleroy, herewith sent you, brought before John Edward Conant Esquire, one of His Majesty's Justices of the Peace in and for the said county, by Samuel

Plank, and charged before me, the said Justice, upon the oath of John Goodchild, and others, with feloniously uttering and publishing as true, in the City of London, a certain false, forged and counterfeited letter of attorney, for the sale of £46,000 reduced three per cent annuities in the capital stock of the Governor and Company of the Bank of England, against the peace of our Sovereign Lord the King, his crown and dignity. Him therefore safely keep in your custody until he shall be discharged by due course of law; and for so doing this shall be your sufficient warrant. Given under my hand and seal the twenty-first of October 1824.' The commitment has been signed by John Conant." Wontner paused and looked at Fauntleroy. "Do you understand the commitment?"

The banker tried to speak, but all that came out was a croak. Wontner poured a cup of water from the jug on his desk and handed it to Fauntleroy, who drank deeply, nodding his thanks before answering, "Yes, I understand it."

Wontner slotted the commitment carefully into the folder, and then clasped his hands on top of it. "I noted as your hackney arrived that that you have brought some items with you, and of course you can take whatever you wish into your cell, but I would strongly advise you to leave here with me anything of particular value. I will issue you a receipt, and ensure that your belongings are passed to your family. You will need some money, of course, for daily disbursements, but beyond that – any rings, perhaps, or your watch?"

Fauntleroy pulled his watch from its pocket, unclipped it, held it for a long moment in his hand, and then handed it to Wontner. The keeper took it and inspected it with a practised eye.

"A fine piece," he said almost to himself. "Swiss mechanism, French case… Forgive me, Mr Fauntleroy – for many years I was a clockmaker, and the interest never wanes. I shall write out a receipt and bring it to you later." He placed the watch carefully in a desk drawer, and stood up. Fauntleroy and Vickery rose to their feet as well. "Mr Fauntleroy," said Wontner, "the time has come for you to bid farewell to Mr Vickery. Constable Plank will accompany us further." He turned to speak directly to Vickery. "Sir, you are hereby relieved of your duties with regard to this prisoner, and I now take full responsibility for his care and confinement." He walked to his office door, opened it and ushered us out into the hallway. Vickery turned to Fauntleroy and held out his hand.

"Goodbye, sir," he said, and walked back to the main door.

Fauntleroy collected himself just in time to call after him, "Thank you, Mr Vickery, for all your kindness." A gust of wind blew around our legs as the door was opened, and then Vickery was gone.

"Come, Mr Fauntleroy, let me show you to your cell," said Wontner, and he led us off down a corridor. The thud of his wooden leg rang off the stone floor but it did not impede his speed or agility and we had to walk smart to keep up with him. Two guards had joined our party and we moved at a clip along a cold passage, with Wontner pointing out landmarks as we went. "The chapel," indicating to the left. "The men's quadrangle," as we emerged into a large walled space. We crossed to the far side of this and climbed a narrow staircase, and as we reached a landing Wontner looked over his shoulder at Fauntleroy. "I have chosen for you one of our more comfortable cells, one of a pair owned by turnkey Harris. The State Apartments I believe they are called, is that not right, gentlemen?"

"Aye, sir," replied one of the guards with a smile. "Good enough for His Majesty."

"Although I doubt he'd fit through the door," added the other.

"Indeed," continued Wontner. "Turnkey Harris and his wife have moved into the smaller of their two rooms to leave you the larger, Mr Fauntleroy, and they are charged with looking after you and your needs." He stopped outside a studded wooden door and banged upon it. It was hauled open by a short, neat man wearing a leather apron. "This is Mr Harris," said Wontner, indicating the turnkey, "and this is where you will be staying."

Harris stepped to one side and the banker walked past him into the cell and looked around.

"Why, sir," said Fauntleroy, "this is most comfortable! I feared a cell smaller than that at Coldbath, and had heard that you would restrain me with irons. I am most grateful to find that this is not the case."

"Oh no, sir," said Wontner. "Your easement has been paid for."

The banker was plainly puzzled. "My easement? Someone has paid for me to be released from irons? Who?"

"Well," started Wontner. "May I sit, Mr Fauntleroy?" I was touched by the way the keeper played along with his prisoner's pretence that this was merely a social call. Fauntleroy nodded, and he and Wontner sat at the small table pushed against one wall of the cell. The two guards had stayed outside, and the turnkey and I stood by the door. The furnishings were certainly an improvement on those in Coldbath: apart from the table and chairs, there was a small armchair with a stool beside it to serve as side table, and a scuffed but perfectly serviceable large rug upon the floor. Most noticeably, this cell had much more light and ventilation than the one in Coldbath, as the window – albeit high in the wall and of course strongly barred – gave onto the outside world. Through it we could hear the metal of carriage-wheels screeching and sparking on the cobblestones, horses neighing and their drivers and riders shouting as they jostled for position in the street, while piemen and newspaper boys called to the passing throng. Prisoners had often told me that it was these daily sights and sounds that they missed so fiercely.

Wontner continued. "Since it was announced in the papers earlier this week that you would be coming here to Newgate, I have had many visitors. They all think most highly of you, sir, and several have offered to pay your garnish and whatever else may be required to make your stay with us as tolerable as may be hoped. Mr Harris will therefore be able to supply you with whatever you may need in the way of books, writing materials, clothes and the like, while his wife will provide food, candles and soap and also do your laundry."

"Indeed we will, sir," confirmed Harris. "You have only to ask."

Wontner nodded. "I particularly counsel you to make thorough and frequent use of the soap, as it tends to put off the lice." As is always the case when lice are mentioned, I felt myself itching and had to clasp my hands together behind my back to stop me scratching. "Talking of visitors: should you wish to receive a visitor, they will have to apply to me and Mr Harris in the usual way – excepting, of course, your lawyer, who can come and go at will." Wontner looked around the cell, for all the world as though he were the manager of an elegant hotel welcoming a favoured guest. "Is there anything else I can do for you now, sir?"

"No, thank you," said Fauntleroy. "It is simply for me to get used to my new surroundings." He and Wontner stood and shook hands in farewell, and Harris held the door open for the keeper and me before following us out. He pulled the door closed behind him, and as we walked away I heard the familiar scraping home of a heavy iron bolt.

As our little party returned to the front of the gaol, the two guards saluted Wontner and returned to other duties. I was going to take my leave but the keeper seemed reluctant to part and held open the door of his office. "I am about to go off duty, constable," he said. "Would you care to join me for a few moments while I finish up?"

When a man needs to speak it is always wise to listen, and I confess that I very much liked John Wontner. He seemed to me a quiet, thoughtful man; his clothing was tidy and well-made, but not elaborate or unduly fashionable, and his gestures were precise and economical. He had a gentle manner of speaking, which had surely calmed many prisoners over the years.

I settled myself on a chair in his office and watched as he cleared the papers from his desk and slid them into a drawer, locking it and putting the key into his waistcoat pocket. He took the white vase from the window-sill, topped it up with water from his jug, and replaced it. Finally, he smiled at me and sat down with a small sigh.

"Sad, is it not, to see a man fall from grace?"

"Indeed it is," I agreed. "For those who are already desperate, the fall is not so far, but I am always surprised when those who have so much are willing to risk it all."

Wontner nodded. "You saw how frightened he was when he arrived? Two years I have been keeper here, and sometimes it still chills even me – that forbidding entrance, those ghastly chains!"

"Is it right that you used to be a marshal?"

"Aye, an upper marshal in the City – I'd be doing that still, I daresay, but my horse threw me and I lost this..." He thumped his wooden leg.

"So you've ended up here, guarding prisoners instead of rounding them up."

"Funny the turns life takes, isn't it?" said Wontner musingly. "But I'm happy here; there's good work to be done."

We sat in silence.

"I'd been looking forward to meeting him, you know – Fauntleroy, I mean," said Wontner suddenly. "The newspapers would have us believe him the most hated man in London, but those of us with an understanding of finance – and a care for the continued success of our country – well, we think differently."

I waited.

"And in his favour, he has accepted full responsibility for what he did, and hasn't tried to pin the blame on anyone else or claim temporary insanity or benefit of clergy. I don't need to tell you what men will do when they are cornered, do I, constable? To my mind, Fauntleroy has shown admirable bravery, and that's rare. And I'll do all I can to make his stay with us as comfortable as possible."

It's a strange thing, sympathy: it doesn't always strike where you would imagine.

# CHAPTER FIFTEEN

# Harmer lays out his plans

## SATURDAY 23ʳᴰ OCTOBER 1824

Three days later, I was summoned back to Newgate by a message from Wontner. Fearing the worst – perhaps Fauntleroy had done himself some harm – I made with all haste to the gaol. I was admitted, and asked to wait in the corridor outside Wontner's office. After a few minutes, the door opened and a robust, well-fed individual with overly rosy cheeks came out and indicated that I should go in. Wontner was slipping some papers into a desk drawer.

"My apologies for keeping you waiting, constable – Cotton is always complaining about something."

"Cotton? The man who just left?"

Wontner nodded. "The Reverend Horace Cotton, Newgate ordinary. He was giving me the latest news on who has been insulting him. It is a long list."

"Not a popular man, then?"

"Not a bad man, as such – and we have both seen plenty of those. No: it's just that Mr Cotton prefers to spend his time with gentleman felons, ignoring the spiritual needs of the poorer prisoners. And his sermons can be, well, let us say uncompromising."

"Has he been arguing with Mr Fauntleroy?" I asked in confusion.

Wontner clapped a hand to his forehead. "Of course! You are wondering why I sent for you – forgive me. It is simply that on his way into Newgate this morning Mr Harmer told me that he has interesting news, and it occurred to me that whatever he has to say might help you with your enquiries. You mentioned the other day that you were curious about what had made Mr Fauntleroy take such risks. Anyway, Mr Harmer is with his client at the moment but he said that he would stop in to see me on his way out." Wontner took out his watch. "We have a quarter hour before he is due to arrive – shall I show you Cotton's chapel?"

It was only a short walk, as the chapel was situated directly behind the keeper's quarters. It was a plain, high-ceilinged room, chilly on that late October morning, with furnishings and fittings that were meagre in the extreme. The pulpit where I assumed Cotton stood and roared was bare and scanty, with stone pillars on either side and a small harmonium in front of it. There was a curtained gallery – "for the female prisoners," explained Wontner – from which they could see the pulpit but not the rows of male prisoners ranged below them on unpainted benches. There was a dingy font, doubtless pressed into hasty service when yet another miserable gaol baby was born, lest it die unchristened. The altar was simply a tottering little table, with the Ten Commandments written on a faded board tacked onto the wall behind it. Most chilling of all, immediately in front of the pulpit was a single black-painted bench enclosed on three sides by shoulder-high black screens so that its occupants could look nowhere but at the preacher.

"The condemned pew," said Wontner. "Each Sunday, those due to be executed in the coming week are placed there. An unnecessary cruelty, I always think, but the chapel is Cotton's domain." He shivered. "Come: let us go and meet Mr Harmer."

We had been waiting only a few minutes back in Wontner's office when there was a loud knock on the door and in came Mr Harmer and Mr Forbes. The former sank into the chair opposite Wontner and gratefully accepted a cup of tea, while the latter perched on a stool by the door and took out a notebook.

"Mr Harmer," said the keeper, "this is Constable Plank, who is taking a particular interest in the case of Mr Fauntleroy."

Harmer looked at me appraisingly, and then half rose from his seat and thrust out his hand. "Of course: I have seen you in Conant's courtroom. So tell me: why this particular interest?"

It was a question I had asked myself many times, but then questions to oneself do not demand an answer. This one did. All three men looked at me expectantly. "I think it is because I am curious about the combination of a new crime with an old mystery," I began. Harmer raised his eyebrows and settled more comfortably into his chair, as though being told a bedtime story at the fireside. "The theft of money is as old as money itself," I continued, "and even before that there was the theft of valuables. But the theft of that which represents money – of pieces of paper that can be exchanged for money – well, there we have something new. Mr Fauntleroy is not accused of going into his bank's vaults and taking money belonging to others, but of changing pieces of paper to make it look as though their money belonged to him. We police officers will have to learn new skills to catch such people."

Harmer nodded. "And the old mystery you mentioned?" he prompted.

"The oldest mystery of all: why?" I replied. "Why does a successful banker – a man with a spotless reputation, a comfortable home and a safe income – risk it all? Was he greedy, or bored, or arrogant, or vengeful? We know what he is accused of, but we do not yet know why he would have done it." I stopped and the room was silent.

After a few moments, Harmer stirred himself. "Well, I think Henry Fauntleroy is lucky to have such a curious and concerned police officer involved with his case. And it seems that he will need every ounce of luck that he can find. For our man intends to plead guilty."

"Guilty?" echoed Wontner in astonishment. "But that means the gallows. The judge will have no choice."

"Indeed," said Harmer, shaking his head, "and Mr Forbes and I have said this to our client in every possible form of words. I have explained to him that – black though it may look – a not guilty plea will at least lead to a trial, which will give him a chance to explain. Then Constable Plank may solve his great mystery." He smiled at me. "Moreover, a trial will allow me to put mitigation, and I was also planning to bring in a parade of worthies to testify to Mr Fauntleroy's impeccable character and doubtless good intent. A guilty plea puts paid to all of that."

There is one very good reason for pleading guilty, I thought – and then realised as the other three turned to look at me that I had actually spoken aloud. I had no choice but to finish. "And that is because you are guilty."

"Do you think he is?" asked Wontner.

Harmer raised a hand to silence any answer I might have given. "With respect, Constable Plank's view is not the one that will matter – he will not be one of the twelve jurymen. As Mr Fauntleroy's lawyer, I must do all I can to persuade him to avail himself of every opportunity provided by the law to clear his name – and, if we cannot do that, at least to avoid the noose. Mr Wontner, may I ask a favour? Mr Forbes and I were going to return to our chambers to assemble our thoughts and determine how best to proceed, but meeting Constable Plank and learning of his rather enlightened approach to this matter has given me an idea. Would you and the constable come with us, now, to speak to Mr Fauntleroy and encourage him to see the benefits of following my legal advice?"

Fauntleroy was surprised to see his lawyer returning so soon, and accompanied by a pack of us, but he was as courteous as always. He welcomed us into his cell as though to his parlour at home, carefully marking his place in the book he had been reading. Mr Harmer explained briefly why we had come to see him, and the banker's face turned stony as he folded his arms.

"According to my brother John, who is also a solicitor," he said stubbornly, "this may not even come to trial – I may not have to enter a plea at all."

"You mean if the jury at the Sessions decides that there is insufficient evidence against you to proceed?" asked Harmer. Fauntleroy nodded. "That is always possible," conceded Harmer, "but in my view the chances are very slight. The governors of the Bank of England will want their pound of flesh, and they have powerful allies. No: they will make sure that the jury returns a true bill and that this goes to trial. And, as I said earlier, that will mean that you can explain everything – it can all come out."

"But that's just it!" Fauntleroy cried in frustration. "How can you ask me to stand the constant intrusion, the endless questions, the sordid scandal of the thing? If I plead guilty, I rob the vultures of their meal."

I caught Mr Harmer's eye and he nodded his permission. "But there, if I may say so, sir, you are wrong," I said. "The public is already interested in you – we cannot undo that. The newspapers are feeding their appetite for daily digests about your case. And so the press men will write a story anyway: either the story of your trial, when you can explain what you did and why, or that of your execution, when they will speculate wildly about your motives."

"You have seen the penny broadsides distributed after such events," added Wontner. "Full of titillation and vicious nonsense – most distressing."

Fauntleroy sat down. We waited.

"As you can imagine," he began at last, "I have not come lightly to this decision. I have been thinking about it a great deal – after all, there are few other diversions in here. I thank you all for your concern, but I am resolved to plead guilty – for I am indeed guilty of what they say. By pleading guilty, I will put an end to the court appearances, the embarrassment for my family and friends – and in particular, the endless speculation by my bank's customers. If I take the guilt on myself, they will know that the bank itself is sound and that my partners are innocent – that the wrongdoing was by my hand, and my hand alone."

"But the problem with such a plea, sir, as I have explained..." said Harmer quietly.

"Is the scaffold really the only outcome?" asked the banker.

Harmer nodded. "For the time being, yes. There are many of us who think that hanging is too severe a punishment for crimes such as yours, and we are petitioning to change the law – with a great deal of public sympathy. But it will take months, probably years, to bring about that change. And until then the public can beg the courts as loudly as they like to spare you, but if you have pleaded guilty to a crime that carries the penalty of death, there is nothing that can be done: the penalty must be applied. A plea of not guilty gives us valuable time, which we can use to lay out the true circumstances behind what happened – which in turn may save you."

We all waited and looked at the banker.

"Mr Fauntleroy," asked Mr Harmer at last, with just a trace of impatience in his voice, "do you wish to hang? If you do, you will be of no use to me in court. Regardless of the plea, I cannot defend a man who does not believe that he deserves to be saved." We all looked at Fauntleroy, who stared down at his hands clutched in his lap. Long seconds passed. Finally the banker spoke quietly.

"I have done terrible things – things that I should not have done. But I did them with the best of intentions: I did them to save my bank and its customers from ruin. I deserve to be punished, but I do not deserve to hang. And if I am hanged, who will be left who can repair the damage that has been done at the bank?" He took a deep breath, placed both hands flat on the table, and then exhaled. "So it seems that I must plead not guilty, and throw myself, as they say, on the mercy of the court."

As we were taking our leave of Wontner, Mr Harmer asked me to accompany him back to his chambers while Mr Forbes raced on ahead with some papers – there was much to be done to prepare for the inevitable trial. We walked down the steps of the gaol and stopped at the foot of them to take a deep breath.

"I never get used to that place," said Mr Harmer, shuddering.

"Nor I," I answered truthfully. We turned into Newgate Street and headed towards Holborn. Despite his girth, Mr Harmer kept up a good pace. "May I ask you about the trial?" I asked.

"I thought that you might," replied the lawyer. "Well, I'll not lie to you, constable: I believe that the prosecution has a strong case. My spies tell me that they have good, clear witnesses, and we already know that they have documentary evidence. Would that we could examine it more closely – but, as you doubtless know, our outmoded and unbalanced system of justice means that we cannot see copies of the depositions sworn against our client. Forbes and I took the best notes we could during the hearings, from those who were called, but it would be preferable to have the actual depositions to study. There may be some of which we know nothing."

"So you cannot be sure who will be called as a witness at the trial, and therefore have no opportunity to make enquiries as to whether they are credible?"

"Indeed," said Harmer grimly. "The facts sworn may even be false, but how are they to be investigated and disproved, unless they be known?"

"It seems that the dice are loaded in favour of the prosecution."

"Loaded, yes – but we can still roll them." He stopped suddenly, and caught my arm to stop me too. "The forgery I suspect can be proven beyond doubt, but as for the uttering – that is where we must focus our attention. We must convince the jury that, although the documents may have been tampered with, they cannot be absolutely certain that Fauntleroy did the tampering. And if they cannot be certain that he did the tampering, then they cannot be certain that he knew that the documents were forged when he presented them... yes, that is how we must proceed." And he clapped me on the shoulder before starting off again.

Impressed though I was by his dissection of the law, I was still uneasy about his advising a guilty man to plead not guilty. I would never have raised such a concern with, say, the lawyer Freshfield, but Harmer seemed to me to be someone who sought to understand the law, rather than simply to apply it unthinkingly.

"Mr Harmer," I asked, "given that Mr Fauntleroy says that he is guilty, and that he wishes to plead guilty, could he not just do so and rely on the mercy of the jury? I believe that juries are losing their appetite for capital punishment."

"Indeed they are," he confirmed. "Sometimes they will even find not guilty when guilt is plain, simply to save a poor unfortunate from the scaffold. But they will not do that in this instance: there is too much at stake here. The newspapers bay for a guilty verdict, while the Bank of England clutches her petticoats about her like a ruined virgin and cries for revenge. The jury will not be able to find our banker not guilty simply because they do not want him to hang – but they may well look for a legitimate excuse not to send him to the scaffold if they do find him guilty. And it is my job to provide them with that excuse."

By now we were approaching the Inns of Court.

"And how do you intend to do that, if I may, sir?"

"I intend to earn my money, constable! There will be two prongs to our defence: first accuracy and then character. Firstly, I will make sure that everything the prosecution witnesses say is completely accurate. If they speculate or elaborate, I will halt them. If they seem uncertain, I will draw attention to their hesitation. If they appear nervous, I will question their reliability. In short, I will do my utmost to make the jury uneasy about believing anything – and if possible everything – they say. Despite this, I am almost certain that they will find our man guilty.

"And secondly – and this where you may be of some excellent help to me, constable – I will show the character of Mr Fauntleroy in the best possible light. Mr Forbes and I will put together a list of those who would be willing to stand up and say that our client is deserving of mercy, that he had the best and most unselfish of motives. We need men of respectability and dignity and worth. I know some myself, who support in principle the abolition of the death penalty and will therefore stand in defence of anyone facing the scaffold, but we will also need others, friends and business acquaintances who have known Fauntleroy for years and found him to be trustworthy and honest. Perhaps during your investigations you will find some such, and can persuade them to speak in court on behalf of my client."

"It seems that everyone is allowed to speak in court except you," I commented. "Tell me, Mr Harmer: how do you rate Mr Fauntleroy's chances? What would you do in his position?"

"If I were in his position, constable, I would despair of finding a lawyer of my own calibre to defend me."

I couldn't help smiling. I can see that you will not venture an opinion, Mr Harmer."

"It is not the job of a lawyer to have his own opinion, constable. It is his job to shape the opinion of others – most specifically, that of the twelve gentlemen of the jury. And that is what I intend to do." Harmer pulled out his watch and looked at it in surprise. "Always late!" He shook my hand vigorously. "Delighted to meet you, Constable Plank." And he ducked in through a stone gateway and was gone.

# CHAPTER SIXTEEN

# The younger brother

MONDAY 25TH OCTOBER 1824

"Thank you for coming, sir," I said as I shook the hand of John Fauntleroy. He shared his elder brother's slight build and colouring, but not his personal vanity: his hair was uncombed, his cuffs were fraying, and I saw as he put his papers on the table that – unlike his brother, who was most particular about his hands – he bit his nails.

"A lad handed me a note outside Newgate, saying that you wished to see me, but I confess that I am mystified as to your interest in my brother's case. You are a police constable, are you not?"

I indicated that he should sit. "I am, sir. I was the officer who arrested your brother, and I was present at his two hearings here in Great Marlborough Street, before the magistrate Mr Conant."

133

"But surely the arrest was the end of your duties as regards my brother?"

"Ordinarily, yes." I paused, trying to assemble the right words. "But from the start Mr Conant felt that there was something that he had not understood, something that – and you will forgive me, sir – something that your brother wished to hide." The lawyer narrowed his eyes slightly but said nothing. I continued. "Mr Harmer also believes that we are not yet party to the whole story about the forgeries of which your brother is accused. And – given his previous good character and the respect he has always enjoyed – both Mr Conant and Mr Harmer are keen to ensure that all possible information is gathered, so that the jury is fully apprised of the situation."

"And your part in this gathering of information?"

"I have been a police constable for many years, sir, and am generally reckoned a good and fair one. Since my participation in the investigation of Philip Whitehead some dozen years ago, I have made something of a study of forgery..."

"Whitehead? Is it his sister who goes daily to the Bank of England, looking for him?"

"Poor woman – she went quite mad with grief after her brother's death." I stopped suddenly, cursing myself for referring to a man hanged for forgery, but the lawyer seemed not to notice. "Anyway, Mr Conant knows of my interest in this type of crime, and asked me to try to find out what I could. And Mr Harmer hopes that my connections in the less savoury parts of town might turn up something of use."

"Indeed. And am I one of those less savoury connections?"

I could see that John Fauntleroy's mind was sharper than his appearance, and that he mistrusted me. Legal training will make a man wary – as will a quarter-century in a constable's uniform.

"Mr Fauntleroy, as I see it, we all have the same objective here: to paint a clear picture of your brother's actions and motives. What the jury does with that picture is beyond the control of any of us, but one thing is certain: if they believe the story that is making the rounds in the newspapers today, Henry Fauntleroy will hang." I could see from his face that my straight talking had hit the mark. "Mr Fauntleroy, will you help me to understand your brother?"

John Fauntleroy looked at me coolly for a few long moments. "Very well, constable," he said at last. "What pains my brother most is not what would most trouble you or me – the discomfort and degradation of his current situation. No: what distresses him beyond all else is hearing and reading that customers of his bank think that he stole from them. What he wants the jury – indeed, the whole country – to know is that his purpose throughout was to maintain the bank for his customers, to protect them from the changes in fortune visited upon the bank itself."

"After the Bank of England refused to extend the bank's credit?"

John Fauntleroy nodded. "He was so angry after that meeting."

"I have met Mr Foster myself, and did not warm to him," I said. "As I understand it from Mr Harmer, now that your brother has accepted that the only sensible course of action is to plead not guilty, we must concentrate our efforts on mitigation – on convincing the jury that, even though they might well have no option but to find him guilty, he is worthy of their mercy." I paused. "Is he worthy of such mercy, Mr Fauntleroy?"

John Fauntleroy flushed – perhaps from anger, or perhaps from shame – and, interestingly, chose not to answer my question, saying instead, "There are many who will stand up and speak of Henry's good character, of his spotless record as a banker and as a man of integrity." I waited. "Charles Forbes, for instance – the politician. And William Wadd." That was a name I knew: Mr Wadd was the king's surgeon, and his recent writing on surgical advances had been much in the press. I wondered how he and the banker had met. "We can also ask Benjamin Wyatt to appear, although he is busy with the work on Apsley House. Wellington is a demanding master, they say."

"So your brother counts these important men among his friends," I said, writing their names in my notebook. "Are they also customers of his bank?"

John Fauntleroy looked awkward. "Constable Plank, you know that I cannot discuss that – not least because I do not know. A banker does not tell anyone, not even his brother, who banks at his house. The interests of his customers are always uppermost in the mind of a banker."

With the lawyer now on the defensive, I felt that there was nothing more to be gained from our meeting – but I had to unseat him from his high horse if he was going to be of any help to his brother in the future. "Not always, Mr Fauntleroy, and not all customers either, otherwise none of us would be in this situation now, would we?"

# CHAPTER SEVENTEEN

# A true bill

## FRIDAY 29TH OCTOBER 1824

At the end of the week, the weather took a turn for the worse. The wind picked up, and leaves swirled and danced about my feet as I walked along High Holborn. Above me, heavy grey clouds scudded across the dusk sky. It was not the sort of day for visiting a dank place like Newgate, and although it is not like me to be so affected by such things I confess that I very nearly did not go into the gaol at all, reasoning that I could find the information I sought – the almost inevitable outcome of the Sessions – from the Old Bailey instead. But just as I passed the stone steps surmounted by those threatening and heavy chains, John Wontner was going in and he spotted me and beckoned me over.

"Waiting to hear about our banker?" he asked as he grasped the railing to haul himself up the steps. "The

Grand Jury won't be finished for a while yet, and I've a runner standing by to bring me their verdict, so you might as well wait in the warm with me. Besides, I've something to show you."

Wontner was right: it was warm in his room. A fire burned in the grate, and a guard brought in a pot of tea and two cups. As I sipped my drink, Wontner opened a desk drawer and leafed through various documents. "Ah – here it is," he said and handed me a letter.

"My dear Mr Hare," it began, in neat writing with occasional flourishes on the capitals, "In the tin box in the strong room is a watch given to me by the House some years back." I glanced at the signature at the bottom, and knew at once the House in question. "I am anxious to give it to a sincere friend of mine. There is no time to consider, and I am sure you will go with my brother to the strong room and let him bring it to me this morning. It has my arms on the back. Yours ever sincere, H Fauntleroy (Friday morning)".

I looked up at Wontner. "Is this the watch Mr Fauntleroy gave to you when he arrived here?"

"The same. I passed it on to his brother, the solicitor, and he must have put it into the strong room at the bank – and now Mr Fauntleroy wishes to have it returned. This Mr Hare is a clerk at the bank, I believe."

"And has the watch been retrieved?"

"Mr John Fauntleroy brought it in earlier this afternoon – he gave me the letter to explain why he was bringing an item of value into the gaol, so that I can add it to the list of the prisoner's effects."

"Why do you think he wants it?"

Wontner shrugged. "Fond memories, perhaps, to distract him from the present. Or maybe he intends to pass it to someone, should things go as they might."

Just as the words fell from his lips there was a knock at the door, and a young lad put his head in.

"Well, Beech?" asked the keeper.

"A true bill, sir – just returned."

"And the trial?"

"Tomorrow morning, sir – ten o'clock."

"May God be with him," breathed Wontner, shaking his head. "For he will need it."

# CHAPTER EIGHTEEN

# An extraordinary document

## SATURDAY 30TH OCTOBER 1824

When I first saw Henry Fauntleroy on the day of his trial, he had aged seemingly overnight. At first I wondered whether he had powdered his hair too enthusiastically, and he caught me looking at him and put a hand to his head self-consciously.

"I fear we are all growing older, constable," he said. "As to my outfit: will it do? I last wore it to my father's funeral."

The plain black trousers, waistcoat and tailcoat hung a little loose on him, thanks to the prison diet, but I reassured him that he looked smart and respectable. His brother John sat silently in the corner of the cell.

The door opened and in rushed Mr Harmer, dressed in a flowing black robe and tightly-curled white wig for his court appearance but still managing to look dishevelled. He nodded at me and shook the hand of his client.

"So here we are," he said. "I just wanted to make sure that you know what is going to happen today."

"I don't think any of us can claim that, can we?" said Fauntleroy, with an attempt at a smile.

"Indeed not, indeed not," agreed Harmer. "I meant rather the routine of the court – timings and so on. Unless your brother has already...?"

John Fauntleroy shook his head. The banker indicated a chair, and Harmer gathered his robe about him and sat down. "As you know, the trial is a public event. Tickets have been sold by the aldermen, and they are already changing hands for a guinea, which at least should keep out the rabble. Alongside curious members of the public there are students of law, keen to see us lawyers in action, and of course the gentlemen of the press."

"When do we go in?" asked Fauntleroy.

"Well," said Harmer, taking out his watch, "it's nearly nine, and the bench will assemble then, so I have to go now."

"Should I come with you?"

"Oh no, not yet. The jury has to be sworn in, and yours is not the first trial of the day. You're wanted in court at ten, so I will send Mr Wontner to collect you then. Meanwhile, gather your thoughts, and Constable Plank will keep an eye on you."

As he left the cell, Mr Harmer beckoned me to follow. "Do not leave him alone for a moment, constable – not one moment. Who knows what a man in his position may do."

Three-quarters of an hour later, John Wontner arrived. "And how are you today, Mr Fauntleroy?" he asked. "Nervous, I shouldn't wonder." The banker nodded. "They tell me that business is proceeding as planned in the courtroom. Any minute now – ah, here he is."

John Forbes came into the cell, slightly breathless, and bowed to us all. "I have been in court, and Mr Harmer has instructed me to come and report on the lie of the land. We've had a chance to see the jury at work; most of them have served before and know what's expected, and there's no-one Mr Harmer would object to. Property-owning men, of course – local merchants and professionals for the most part, one or two shopkeepers. Today's recorder, Mr Arabin, is a stickler for detail and he'll see that it all runs smoothly."

"And the bench?" asked Mr Wontner.

"Ah yes, the bench. Well, the senior judge is Mr Justice Park." Forbes and Wontner exchanged glances.

"What do you know of him?" asked Fauntleroy, looking from one man to the other.

"Well," began Wontner carefully, "he is what you might term a traditionalist. You will know him from his extremely long nose. And – if we are unlucky – his extremely short temper. When his own son was called to the bar and appeared in his father's court wearing the new style of wig, the old man affected not to recognise him. But in terms of his judgments, Park is a fair and sensible man. Who sits with him?"

"Robert Waithman – the Lord Mayor – and Sir William Garrow," replied Forbes.

"Garrow?" said John Fauntleroy. "But he's for the death penalty!"

"Not entirely," said Forbes quickly. "He holds that it should be allowed as a punishment, but that it should not be mandatory for any crime – that its use should be at the discretion of the jury and the Crown." The brothers looked a little reassured. "The Lord Mayor is of no consequence: he's allowed to be there as an observer but can't take part in proceedings. So, Mr Fauntleroy, do you have any more questions before we proceed to court?" The banker shook his head. "In that case, I think we should go."

Fauntleroy turned to his brother and the two men embraced fiercely.

"I will be in court, Henry – the alderman has reserved a place for me," said John. "I have asked him to position me so that I shall not distract you, but so that you can see me if you wish."

The banker clasped his brother's hands. "Thoughtful as always, my dearest John."

Our footsteps rang in my ears as we left Fauntleroy's cell, went down a stone staircase and then walked through the stone corridor alongside the men's quadrangle of the gaol. We stopped before a heavy wooden door, and a guard came forward and unlocked it with a large key hanging from a chain at his waist. He hauled open the door and we passed into an enclosed passage.

"A shortcut to the Sessions House – the Old Bailey," explained Mr Wontner.

"Ah," said the banker in disappointment, "I was hoping that we would be going outside, if only to cross the road."

At the other end of the passage, we stood aside to let the guard unlock the door and then go ahead to check that the court was ready to receive us. It was five minutes past ten. The guard reappeared and beckoned to us, and we entered the courtroom: first Fauntleroy and Mr Forbes, and then Mr Wontner and me.

My eyes having become accustomed to the half-light of the stone passageway, I was momentarily dazzled by the inverted mirror suspended over the dock, so positioned as to reflect light from the windows onto the face of the accused. Mr Forbes indicated that Fauntleroy should step into the dock, while he himself walked to the barristers' table. Mr Wontner and I took up our usual positions on either side of the dock. Fauntleroy tried to bow to the bench, but his knees gave way and he almost fell backwards. He grasped the bar with trembling hands, bent his head and took several deep breaths. After a few moments, he was able to look up at the three men on the bench.

Beneath the large gilded sword of justice fixed onto the crimson wall sat the Lord Mayor. Robert Waithman was a tall, spare fellow with luxuriant side-whiskers and sad brown eyes. He was wearing a blue and furred gown, with his chain of office around his neck. With the red background, the blue robe and the glinting chain and sword, the effect was almost theatrical. To the left of the mayor sat Sir William Garrow, a serious-looking man in his sixties wearing his judge's wig with stiff-necked pride and looking out over the court with detachment. On the other side of the Mayor was the senior judge, Sir James Park. His nose was indeed remarkably long.

The lawyers gathered at the barristers' table were like a flock of ravens in their black gowns. I recognised the Attorney General John Copley, who led the prosecution team. With thick, dark, curly hair showing beneath his snowy-white wig, pale blue eyes and a deep dimple in his chin, Copley would have been a striking man, but his rather pursed lips gave him a fussy, spoilt expression. Alongside Copley were his two associates – "Bolland and Bosanquet, like a variety act!" whispered Mr Wontner to me.

A clerk stood, cleared his throat and started to read. "Henry Fauntleroy, you stand indicted, for that you on the first of June, in the fifty-fifth year of the late King, in the parish of St Marylebone, did feloniously and falsely make and forge and counterfeit a certain deed, purporting to bear the name of Frances Young, for the transfer of £5,450 long annuities of her monies, in the stocks established by the Act of the Fifth of the late King George the Second with intent to defraud the said Frances Young of the said stock."

He then enumerated six individual counts within the indictment before turning to face the dock and asking, "Henry Fauntleroy, how say you? Are you guilty or not guilty of the said felony?"

All eyes turned to look at the banker. After a pause, and in a voice so faint that it was almost a whisper, he replied, "Not guilty." The two judges made a note of his response, their pens moving exactly in time with each other.

"How will you be tried?"

Fauntleroy looked confused, and Wontner leaned up to prompt him. "By God and my country," said the banker.

As the clerk read out more indictments, I looked at my surroundings. For a room with such a large reputation, the dimensions of the Old Bailey were surprisingly small, almost intimate. The large sash windows at the back of the court allowed plenty of light into the room, even this late in the year. Tall, elegant Doric columns held up the ceiling above the galleries, and four brass chandeliers hung low above the centre of the court. To my right sat the jury, surrounded by shoulder-high wooden panels to protect them from being distracted – or influenced – by anything but the case before them. They were neatly arranged in three tiered rows, like toy soldiers in a box, with a clear view of both the accused and the bench, and they occasionally made notes on paper set on the little desks before them. Opposite the jury sat the privileged visitors; among them I spotted Buller and Richards from the Bank of England. Just behind them, as he had promised his brother, sat John Fauntleroy.

The reading of the indictments, each with many counts, took a full twenty-five minutes, and to each Fauntleroy pleaded not guilty and put himself for trial by God and his country. After all of the pleas had been recorded, the clerk raised his arm to point at the jury. "Henry Fauntleroy," he said, "these good men are to pass between our Sovereign Lord the King, and you, life and judgment."

Everyone turned to look at the jury. How ordinary they appeared, the dozen gentlemen, professionals and merchants. One was suffering from a heavy cold and sneezed frequently and loudly into a handkerchief held to his nose; another – to my eye, the youngest of the twelve – was clearly more interested in the various ladies in court than in the trial at hand. And yet they and their fellows were now all that stood between Fauntleroy and the scaffold.

At a signal from Mr Justice Park, Fauntleroy collapsed into the chair in the dock and the prosecution began its case. John Copley rose to his feet. "The prisoner at the bar," and he indicated Fauntleroy with a dismissive wave, as though the banker were a nuisance, "is charged with feloniously forging a power of attorney for the sale of certain stock standing in the books of the Bank of England in the name of Frances Young. He is also charged with uttering that power of attorney, knowing it to be forged. It is my duty today to lay before you the evidence in support of these charges." He paused dramatically; having watched plenty of barristers in my time, I recognised the method. "If you have formed any impressions that are unfavourable to the prisoner, I urge you to dismiss them from your recollection and concentrate solely upon the evidence. Moreover, although you have already heard that there are other charges against the prisoner, he has a right to be tried upon the charge before you now as if it were the only one, without reference to any other." Copley halted again, and several law students scribbled furiously.

"The prisoner at the bar," continued Copley, "is a partner in the banking house of Marsh and Company. The house was established thirty years ago, with the father of the prisoner taken into it as a partner on its formation and rising to become managing partner. In the year 1807, Mr Fauntleroy, the father, died, and his situation was immediately occupied by his son, the prisoner at the bar. From that time, almost the whole business of the bank devolved upon him, owing to his great experience in business, his practical knowledge of its details, and his comparative superiority in those respects over the rest of his partners, who were almost totally unacquainted with commercial transactions.

"In the year 1815, a lady by the name of Frances Young, residing at Chichester, was a customer of the house. She had an account with them, and the house had a power of attorney from her to receive the dividends upon her stock – but not to transfer or sell the principal of it. In June 1815, an application was made at the Bank of England to sell £5,000 of her stock by her power of attorney. This power of attorney purported to be signed and executed by Frances Young in May 1815, but her signature was a forgery, as she had never made any such instrument. A forgery!" Copley thumped the barristers' table, driving home his point. "Her signature was attested by two witnesses – John Watson and James Tyson, clerks to the house of Marsh and Company. Those attestations were also forgeries." He thumped the table again. "Neither of these individuals ever saw any such instrument executed, and at that time had never seen Frances Young."

Copley then held up both hands, as though halting a runaway carriage. "Even supposing the case rested here, it is pregnant with the most powerful and conclusive evidence against the prisoner." He paused. "There is, however, a document of character so extraordinary, so perfectly unparalleled, and so conclusive in its effects as to leave not the shadow of a doubt as to the part taken in this transaction by the prisoner at the bar."

I looked across at Wontner, and he shook his head and gave a small shrug. Copley – who they say used to attend the theatre to learn from the actors – allowed the pause this time to stretch. Several of the jurymen leaned forward in their seats. Copley eventually continued.

"When the prisoner was apprehended in his own counting-house, he locked his private desk with a key that was attached to his watch. That key was taken from him by the officer who apprehended him, who gave it to the respectable solicitor for the Bank of England," and here Copley indicated Freshfield, "who went to the premises in Berners Street to search among the prisoner's papers in order to ascertain from them, if possible, the part he had taken in this forgery. One of the back rooms of the counting-house is a parlour, reserved for the use of the partners of the bank and their visitors." Copley's tone was that of a genial fireside storyteller. "In that room, which contained several tin cases for the storage of title deeds, Mr Freshfield saw one tin case without a name upon it. The key which had been taken from the prisoner opened his private desk. In that desk was found another key, which opened the tin case. And in that tin case were many papers belonging to the prisoner, among them this extraordinary document."

Copley held out his hand wordlessly, and one of his colleagues stood and ceremoniously handed him a folded sheet of paper. With great care, Copley unfolded the paper slowly, shook it out, turned it to the light and proceeded to describe it.

"This document is divided into columns, giving the names of customers of the bank, and the amount of their stock sold by the prisoner at the bar. First among them, I see Miss Frances Young – you have already heard of her, and shall hear more. Here is Mrs Elizabeth Fauntleroy, the prisoner's own mother, and his elderly uncle Mr Jedediah Kerie. Further down we have Lady Nelson, for whom the prisoner sold..." he affected to check the sheet and widened his eyes with pantomime surprise, "£11,595 of Consols." There were gasps. "More names, more money... finishing with Lord Aboyne, and £61,550 of four per cents." There were cries of "How much did he say?" and "A fortune!" Copley continued as though nothing had happened. "According to my arithmetic, that makes a total of upwards of £170,000. The whole of this document is in the handwriting of the prisoner, as are these next words." Copley waited until the court was completely silent, and then read the next sentences in a clear, measured voice.

"'In order to keep up the credit of our house, I have forged powers of attorney and have sold out all the above sums, without the knowledge of any of my partners. I have given the different accounts credit for the dividends as they became due, but have never posted them.' There then follows this signature: 'H Fauntleroy, Berners Street, the seventh of May 1816'." Copley looked up from the sheet of paper in his hand and turned his level gaze to the jury before repeating slowly, "I have forged powers of attorney."

There was a moment's shocked silence in the courtroom, and then voices erupted everywhere. I looked at Fauntleroy, who had turned whiter even than his usual prison pallor. Reaching over the bar, his hand grasped my shoulder like a claw. "That was my own private document – my own reckoning," he hissed. "How else could I repay them if not by keeping a record?"

At the barristers' table, I saw an alarming sight: Mr Harmer and Mr Forbes were closing their books.

Copley carried on, shaking his head. "A more extraordinary document to be discovered under such circumstances never existed. Was there ever a record of fraud more intelligible?" Copley laid down the paper with great reverence and sighed deeply with mock regret before continuing in a more natural voice. "It is now my duty to trace this forgery from commencement to conclusion."

This he proceeded to do. He told of the original sale of Miss Young's stock, and how Fauntleroy had posted the profit from that sale to his own private account at the bank. He promised to bring witnesses before the court to testify that Miss Young had not ordered the sale of her stock, and that the instrument used to effect that sale was forged – and moreover that the handwriting on the forged instrument was that of Henry Fauntleroy.

The first witness for the prosecution was James Tyson. John Bosanquet, the prosecution lawyer who stood to question him, had the look of a country gentleman, with untidy fair hair beneath his wig, large capable hands and a ready smile. Tyson confirmed that in 1815 Fauntleroy had been the managing partner at Marsh and Company.

"And what are the duties of the managing partner?" probed Bosanquet.

"It varies from house to house," said Tyson, "but at our house, it meant that Mr Fauntleroy was the active partner. He transacted the principal business of the house."

And so, neatly, the prosecution demonstrated that Fauntleroy's decisions were his alone.

As at the hearing, the power of attorney was then handed to Tyson.

"What do you see on this document, Mr Tyson?" asked the lawyer.

"I see my name given as a witness, and after the signature J Tyson are the words 'clerk to Marsh and Company, bankers, Berners Street'."

"Are those words in your handwriting?"

In recent days, newspaper reports had described Tyson as both "the banker's closest ally" and "the prisoner's dupe", so people were curious to hear what he would say. Would he back his friend?

"No, sir – it is not my handwriting."

"If it is not your handwriting, whose do you think it is?" Tyson looked down at the document but said nothing. "The handwriting, if you please, Mr Tyson. Look at it. Remember that you are under oath."

Tyson spoke so quietly that the judges had to lean forward to catch his reply. "I think that it is in Mr Fauntleroy's handwriting. It is like his character."

"And how do you know his character?" asked Bosanquet.

"As his clerk, sir, I have been much in the habit of seeing him write."

Bosanquet nodded at Tyson and then returned to his seat at the barristers' table. Tyson was released from the witness box, and as he passed the dock I could see that his eyes were red-rimmed and smudged with strain and fatigue.

The next witness was Robert Browning, who confirmed that he worked, and had worked for many years, in the three per cent Consols office of the Bank of England. He too was handed the power of attorney. "Yes, I am a witness to this instrument. I remember the prisoner bringing it to the bank, and I saw the signature 'H Fauntleroy' written by the prisoner. I recorded the transaction in the bank book and the transfer book." A ledger was placed in front of Browning, and he turned to a page marked by a slip of paper. "Yes, this is it, in the transfer book. We sold the stock to William Flower, a stockbroker. And here, next to it: the signature of Henry Fauntleroy."

Deciding that the jury had heard enough of dry documents, Copley turned to the bench. "We propose now, my Lord, to call Miss Frances Young."

As Copley had hoped, Miss Young's arrival in court caused a great stir, and Mr Justice Park had to call for silence several times once she had reached the witness box. A slight woman with fair hair tucked into a plain bonnet, she looked pale but composed, holding her head high. I estimated her to be thirty years of age. Asked about her holdings of stock in 1815, she replied in a quiet but steady voice, "I had then three per cent Consols to the amount of £5,450. Marsh and Company received the dividends on that stock for me. A short while back, I purchased £100 more, and since then have regularly received dividends on £5,550."

"But surely you instructed your bank to sell some £5,000 of stock in June 1815? Using this power of attorney signed the previous month?" queried Copley innocently, handing her the instrument.

"Oh no, I never authorised the bank to make such a sale," replied Miss Young. "I never executed this instrument. The signature, Frances Young, is not my writing." She passed the document back to the lawyer and a rattle of whispering ran around the court.

"Are you certain?" queried Copley. "Would you like to look again at the instrument? This is very important, very important indeed."

"I am entirely certain," replied Miss Young, holding herself upright. "I never authorised the prisoner, or any other person, to sell out £5,000 for me. Anyway, I was never in London in May of 1815 to sign such an instrument – I was all that spring in Chichester."

Copley thanked Miss Young before gallantly offering her his arm as she stepped down from the witness box and escorting her from the court. She did not once look at Fauntleroy. Copley returned to the barristers' table and said, with no small satisfaction in his voice, "That, my Lords, concludes the case for the prosecution."

To my left, a woman in the public gallery remarked loudly to her neighbour, "Well, it's hard to imagine what else we need to hear. The scoundrel's as good as hanged already."

# CHAPTER NINETEEN

# The parade of worthies

## SATURDAY 30TH OCTOBER 1824

Mr Justice Park looked across at the dock and spoke in measured tones. "Prisoner, the case on the part of the prosecution being closed, you may, if you wish, say anything you think proper to the jury or to me." As one, every head in the court turned to look at Fauntleroy. He rose slowly to his feet, leaning on the bar for support, and pulled a sheaf of cream papers covered in his neat handwriting from his coat pocket. He put on his spectacles and adjusted them.

"My Lords," said the banker, "I will trouble you with a few words." A tear ran down his cheek and he wiped it away with the back of his hand before straightening the papers and starting to read in a voice so low that at times it was almost inaudible. "My Lords and gentlemen of the jury, I will endeavour to explain the embarrassments of the banking house in which I have been for many years the active and only responsible partner. Although I may be unable to secure my liberation by a verdict of the jury, yet they may be considered as some extenuation of the crimes of which I stand accused." The papers in Fauntleroy's hands trembled and fluttered.

"My father established the banking house in 1792, in conjunction with Mr William Marsh and some other gentlemen. Two of the partners retired in 1794, at which time a loss of £20,000 was sustained. Here commenced the difficulties of the house. In 1800 I became a clerk in the house and continued so for six years, and the firm was so well satisfied with my attention and zeal for the interest and welfare of the establishment that I was handsomely rewarded by them. In 1807 my father died and I succeeded him as managing partner. At this time I was only twenty-two years of age, and the entire weight of a needy banking establishment at once devolved upon me." Fauntleroy paused, and closed his eyes as though remembering something dreadful. "Once in charge, I found the house deeply involved in advances to builders and others. In 1814, 1815 and 1816, our house was called upon to provide more than £100,000 to avert losses."

Several people drew in their breath at the mention of the vast sum.

Fauntleroy continued. "In 1819 one of our partners died, and we were called upon to pay over his capital. The house was by now nearly without resources. The whole burden of management falling upon me, I was driven to a state of distraction and, almost broken-hearted, I sought resources where I could. And so long as such resources were provided, and the credit of the house was supported, no enquiries were made by my partners either as to the manner in which they were procured, or as to the sources whence they were derived."

At this point, the banker stood up taller and for the first time looked directly at the jury. "I declare that all the monies temporarily raised by me were applied not in one instance to my own purposes, but in every case they were immediately placed to the credit of the banking house, and applied to the payment of the pressing demands upon it. I never had any advantage beyond that in which all my partners participated. They have considered themselves as partners only in the profits — and I am to be burdened with the whole of the opprobrium, that others may consider them as the victims of my extravagance. I do not mean to incriminate others, nor to excuse myself, but I will not consent to be held up to the world as a cold-blooded and abandoned profligate, ruining all around me, and involving even my confiding partners in the general destruction!" Taking a deep breath, the banker calmed himself. "I fully rely that you, gentlemen of the jury, will give an impartial and merciful decision." Fauntleroy bowed to the foreman of the jury and then to the bench before sinking into his seat.

Mr Justice Park nodded to Mr Harmer, who rose to his feet. "It is now my honour to call forward sixteen worthy gentlemen who would like to speak on behalf of Mr Fauntleroy," said the lawyer, "to testify to his excellent character, upstanding nature and great respectability. Several of these gentlemen are public figures themselves, and all have known – and trusted – Mr Fauntleroy for many years."

Sixteen seemed to me rather excessive, but although I found some of them unremarkable and unmemorable, others do stick in the mind. Sir Charles Forbes, for instance, was a well-known merchant in Bombay, recently created a baronet, and had a booming voice impossible to ignore.

"I have known Fauntleroy for twelve years," he said. "I have always considered him an honourable, benevolent, obliging gentleman."

"Is Mr Fauntleroy simply a friend?" asked Harmer. "Or do you have knowledge of him as a banker?"

"He is my banker – and in that capacity he is an able, attentive and upright man of business."

The prominent wine merchant Divie Robertson confirmed that he had been friends with Fauntleroy for over a decade, during which time the banker had maintained "as high a character as a man could possess", while William Wadd, the king's surgeon, declared that Fauntleroy had "a most excellent character, possessed of kind and honourable feelings".

One witness familiar to me but probably not to many others in attendance was Anthony Brown.

"What is your occupation, sir?" asked Harmer.

"I am a sheriff of London," replied Brown.

"A sheriff? By which you mean the person who attends the justices on the bench in this very court?" Brown nodded. "A most responsible and trustworthy position, to be held only by a man who has the best interests of justice at heart," mused Harmer, as though to himself but loudly enough for everyone to hear. "To the matter before us today. How long have you known Mr Fauntleroy?"

"I have known the prisoner at the bar for seventeen years."

"And what opinion have you formed of him over your long acquaintance?"

"I have always entertained the highest opinion of his talents as a man of business, and the greatest confidence in his integrity as a man of honour."

Benjamin Wyatt was introduced to the court as "the esteemed architect, currently working for the Duke of

Wellington on his London home"; Harmer certainly knew how to wring the best value from a witness.

"And is it through your work that you met Mr Fauntleroy?" asked Harmer.

"Originally, yes – about twelve years ago now. We both had business connections with the building trade, but we soon found that we had more in common than this and so we became friends."

"And what is your opinion of his character?"

Wyatt looked across at the banker. The crowd waited for his response. "Throughout our friendship, our long and valued friendship," replied Wyatt at last, "Henry Fauntleroy has been honourable, kind-hearted and benevolent."

Harmer's final witness was led to the stand and took the oath as Joseph Bushnan, Comptroller of the Chamber of London.

"Comptroller – that is a financial position, is it not?" asked Harmer.

"Very much so."

"So as a comptroller you would have to be aware of financial matters, and to have complete integrity in conducting them?"

"Indeed," replied Bushnan.

"And how long have you known Mr Fauntleroy?"

"About fifteen years, I should say."

"And do you," asked Harmer, pausing between phrases, "as another man of finance," another pause, "and integrity," pause, "consider him honest?"

Taking his cue from the lawyer, Bushnan answered in equally measured tones. "I have always considered Henry Fauntleroy to be perfectly honest and honourable." He turned to look directly at the foreman of the jury. "Perfectly honest and honourable," he repeated.

Once Bushnan had returned to his seat and the court had settled, Mr Justice Park addressed the jury. "Gentlemen: the prisoner before you is indicted for forging a power of attorney to procure the transfer of stock belonging to Miss Frances Young, and for uttering this power of attorney, knowing it to be forged." He glanced down at the papers in front of him and then back up at the jury, looking deliberately along the rows of men. "Now, I must speak to you about information in the public prints. If they have propagated misrepresentations to the disadvantage of the prisoner before his trial, it is a most cruel thing. However, I am confident that you will pay no attention to anything you had ever heard respecting the prisoner's conduct before you took the book into your hands, by which you bound yourselves, before God, to deliver a true verdict according to the evidence."

The judge now held up a single index finger. "The only point you have to decide is this: did the prisoner know this power of attorney to be forged and utter it with intent to defraud the Bank of England or Frances Young? In reaching your decision, there are three questions for your consideration. The first is: are you satisfied that the instrument was forged, or not? If it was not forged, the charge falls to the ground at once. If it was forged, then comes the second question: did the prisoner utter it, aye or no? Then, if it was forged and he did utter it, comes the third and most important question: did he know it to be a forgery? If you are satisfied that the forgery, the uttering and the guilty knowledge are all substantiated by the evidence, there can be no doubt of the guilt of the prisoner and you must return a verdict against him.

"On the first question: was the instrument forged? Miss Young proved that the name 'Frances Young' signed to the power of attorney produced was not in her handwriting, and that she had never authorised any person to write it. The two clerks likewise proved that their names were not in their handwriting and that they had never seen Miss Young in their lives until the start of these proceedings. This is as strong evidence that the instrument is a forgery as can be produced.

"The next question for your consideration is: did the prisoner utter the false instrument? Robert Browning swore that he saw the prisoner sign and execute the instrument. The transfer of stock was made by the Bank of

England upon a power of attorney presented by the prisoner, the Bank supposing it to be a genuine instrument. If I had myself any doubts I would be glad to suggest them, but I really think that the evidence proves beyond all possibility of doubt that the prisoner uttered the instrument.

"The third question is: did the prisoner at the time of uttering know that the instrument was a forgery? It has been proved that, although the transfer of stock took place in June of 1815, the prisoner continues to this day to give Miss Young credit for its amount in lists of stock on which dividends are to be received. This suggests that he has tried to conceal the fact of the sale.

"But above all we have this." Mr Justice Park sifted through the pile of papers before him, extracted a document, and held it up. It was Fauntleroy's own reckoning of amounts. "This document is the most extraordinary document that has ever been produced, during all the long annals of crime, in a court of justice. I have never in the whole course of my life either read or heard of so singular a paper. It is perfectly unparalleled." He waved the document at the jury. "Is it possible for any man to say, after this evidence, that there can be any doubt that at the time the prisoner uttered the power of attorney he knew it to be forged? Why, he solemnly declared the fact under his own hand eight years ago!" He shook his head in disbelief. "I think that, after what this day has been proved in court, there can be no doubt that this forgery was committed with intent to defraud."

Mr Justice Park laid down the piece of paper and continued in a quieter voice. "There is one point in the prisoner's favour which I am glad of: a great number of respectable gentlemen – with some of whom I am myself acquainted – have given him the highest character for integrity and honour." The judge sighed with regret. "If you are satisfied by the evidence you have heard that the crime imputed to the prisoner has been proved, it will be your duty to find him guilty. If you entertain any doubt as to the prisoner's guilt, you will fling the weight of his character into the scale and will acquit him. If, however, you entertain no doubt, then you must discharge your duty with firmness and consistency and must return a verdict of guilty against him."

The court was silent, save for the noise of pens scratching across paper as journalists and jurymen alike made notes of the judge's directions. Then the twelve men of the jury rose to their feet, filed out of the jury box and left the courtroom. The three men on the bench likewise departed. I glanced at my watch: it was ten minutes to two o'clock. Nearly four hours – the gawpers were certainly getting their value for money from this trial, as even murder trials rarely took longer than twenty minutes. No wonder I was so hungry, and others must have felt the same for they reached into bags and baskets for slices of pie, heels of bread and small flagons of drink. Harmer walked across to Fauntleroy and reached up to touch his arm. "Courage, sir," he said.

The door to the court opened, and a guard signalled over the heads of the crowd to the clerk at the front of the room. "They're recalling the bench," said Wontner, "so the jury is ready to return." I was astonished: they had been gone only fifteen minutes – hardly enough time to decide on one's supper, let alone a man's life. The jury and then the judges walked back into court, and people hurriedly packed away their picnics, brushing crumbs from their mouths and their clothes.

When eleven jurymen had sat down and only the foreman remained standing, Mr Justice Park nodded at the clerk. He in turn looked at the foreman and asked him, "How say you: are you agreed upon your verdict?"

"We are agreed."

"Is the prisoner at the bar guilty or not guilty?"

I made sure to watch the banker as the verdict was pronounced.

"Guilty of uttering the forged instrument, knowing it to be forged."

"Dear God, no!" cried Fauntleroy – but not before the smallest, the most fleeting of smiles had appeared on his lips. Although who is to say how any of us might react on hearing such a pronouncement?

# CHAPTER TWENTY

# Three weapons

SATURDAY 30ᵀᴴ OCTOBER 1824

"Forgive me, sir," said John Wontner, as he crouched in front of the armchair. Between us, he and I had all but carried the banker from the courtroom, back along the stone passageways, and finally propped him in the armchair in his cell. He was crying and howling, great racking sobs tearing from him as his fists pounded the arms of his seat. "Forgive me," said Wontner again, and slapped Fauntleroy hard, twice. The noise stopped as though someone had slammed shut a window. Wontner walked over to Harmer and John Fauntleroy who were standing by the door. "'Tis the shock, making him like that. He'll be better now."

The banker looked up at us, his eyes red and his cheeks wet. "Better?" he said with incredulity. "How in God's name could I be better? I have just been told that I am to die."

Harmer sat in one of the chairs and then pulled it so close to his client that their knees were almost touching. "That may well be your interpretation," he said urgently, "but it is not mine. And as you are merely a banker while I am a lawyer and therefore know more of these matters, I suggest that you listen to me."

John Fauntleroy and Wontner sat, while I took up my usual position as sentry by the door.

"I will not deny that I was hoping for a different outcome," continued Harmer. "It would have made my job considerably easier if the jury had acquitted you – or if you had mentioned that little document of yours. But I can tell you now that it was always going to be a long shot..."

Fauntleroy leapt to his feet. "You knew that they would find me guilty?" he yelped. "You knew – and yet you made me go through the charade, no, the torment of that trial?"

Harmer laid a hand on the banker's arm. "Please, Henry, sit. Please." Fauntleroy clenched his fists, but did as he was asked.

"Listen to me carefully, Henry," continued Harmer. "If you had pleaded guilty, you would have gone straight to the scaffold, is that not so?"

"Indeed – and that is where I am heading now, but after a great deal more fuss, and considerable expense," said the banker gracelessly.

Harmer held up a hand to silence him. "But by pleading not guilty, you were able to have a trial which – though an ordeal – gave us the opportunity to explain your motives and to bring forward many respectable witnesses to speak for you. We could do this only because we went to trial, is that not so?" Fauntleroy nodded. "So now you have been found guilty and will be sentenced. The sentence, I warn you, is a foregone conclusion: uttering is still, much to my disgust, a capital offence." John Fauntleroy made a sharp intake of breath but said nothing. Harmer continued again. "But the beauty of this is that we know what we are up against, so we already know how to frame our responses."

"Our responses?" echoed Fauntleroy.

"Of course," replied Harmer. "The trial was only the first of three weapons at our disposal." He held up three fingers, and then turned down one of them with his other hand. "The first was the trial – that's gone. Next we shall make a motion in arrest of judgment. In other words, we shall argue that the trial was not conducted correctly."

"Was it not?" asked Fauntleroy, looking across at his brother, who made no reply.

"Well, my learned friend Mr Alley believes that he has found something to our advantage, and has already lodged a request with the clerk that he be allowed to address the bench before sentencing on Tuesday. Mr Alley is an energetic advocate, and he makes a close study of the criminal law, so I am minded to give him his head. So we have the motion in arrest of judgment as our second weapon." Harmer turned down a second finger, leaving just one standing.

"And the third?" asked John Fauntleroy.

"As you know," replied Harmer, "the prerogative of mercy rests with the Crown – and that is where we shall go."

"To the King?" asked the banker.

"Should it be necessary, yes. We shall recommend you to the royal clemency and seek to obtain a pardon from the King. We must start work straight away – just in case – on our petition. But for now, Henry, I shall leave you with your brother, as I am sure that you have family matters to discuss."

# CHAPTER TWENTY-ONE

# Acts and deeds

## TUESDAY 2ND NOVEMBER 1824

Over the next days the newspapers were full of accounts of the trial. Some gloated and bayed for blood, while others conducted earnest debates about what this meant for the reputation of London's banks. I glanced through some of the less sensational and scaremongering of them as I waited in the police office before heading off to the Old Bailey once again the following Tuesday. A small advertisement in one of the papers caught my eye. "Robbed by Mr Henry Fauntleroy?" asked the headline. The notice went on to explain that a new banking house – Sir Samuel Scott, Bart and Company – had been set up in Holles Street to assist customers of Marsh and Company who might wish to move away from the tainted bank. As an incentive, the new house was offering a bounty of ten shillings in the pound on all accounts moved. I rather wished I had an account myself, for such a reward.

As at the trial, Wontner, Harmer and I accompanied Fauntleroy into the courtroom to hear his lawyers put their motion in arrest of judgment. On the bench were Sir William Garrow and Mr Newman Knowlys.

"Knowlys is the recorder," Wontner explained quietly as Fauntleroy stepped up into the dock. "The most senior permanent judge of this court. He's used for sentences, and Garrow is here to represent your trial. Park is away on the circuit."

Peter Alley, at the barristers' table, stood and addressed the bench. "Your Lordships, I mean today to move in arrest of judgment on the part of Henry Fauntleroy."

Garrow nodded. The clerk turned to Fauntleroy and intoned, "What do you have to say that you should not die according to law, having been convicted of a felony?"

Fauntleroy remained silent, as Harmer had warned him to, and Alley replied instead. "I am to address the court on the part of the prisoner. Your Lordships are doubtless aware that the conviction of the prisoner took place on an indictment charging him with having uttered a forged power of attorney, knowing it to be forged at the time of uttering it." Alley looked up at the judges, both of whom looked back impassively. "It is claimed that there is an express Act of Parliament which makes forging a power of attorney a capital offence. However, although by the eighth year of George the First it was a capital offence to forge a bond or security for money, that penalty did not extend to the act of uttering such an instrument." Alley glanced at the notes ranged before him on the table, and his fellow lawyer William Brodrick handed him a sheet. "By a subsequent Act, in the fourth year of George the Second, it was made a capital offence to forge certain instruments therein enumerated, which included deeds but not powers of attorney. By the fifty-seventh year of George the Third – a mere eight years ago – it was made a capital offence to forge a power of attorney to obtain a seaman's wages, or to utter such a forged instrument knowing it to be a counterfeit. That Act demonstrated that it was not the intention of the legislature that to forge a power of attorney was a capital offence under the two earlier statutes, for, if so, what was the use of the fresh enactment?"

I tried to follow the argument, but the parade of Georges and Acts started to merge into one. I glanced at Harmer, who was leaning forward, his eyes shielded by a hand, ostensibly consulting a book open on the table in front of him; I suspected he was dozing.

Alley continued for a little longer, and then Brodrick stood. "I wish to make a few observations in support of what has been so ably stated by my learned friend. The verdict of the jury was not that of guilty generally, but guilty of uttering a forged instrument, knowing it to be forged. And the object of our present motion is not that there should be no judgment at all, but that there should be no judgment of death. The second and third counts of the indictment referred to the forged instrument as a 'deed'. The question is whether a power of attorney is actually a deed within the meaning of the Act passed in the reign of George the Second, which is the Act that makes the forging of deeds a capital offence, but not the forging of powers of attorney. I believe that I shall be able to prove that the Legislature did not so consider it."

Ah – this might be something, I thought. Fauntleroy too seemed to take more interest, leaning forward in his chair.

"The law passed in the fifty-seventh year of George the Third, to which my learned brother has referred, alludes to the forging and uttering, amongst other things, of a power of attorney for obtaining seaman's wages. Why specify 'power of attorney', if a power of attorney was already included by the word 'deed' in the earlier law passed in the fourth year of George the Second – which is the statute upon which this current indictment was framed. A power of attorney, to my mind, is not a deed but a mere authority to another person to act. As it is not a deed, it is not caught by the statute, and so the current indictment cannot stand." Brodrick bowed to the judges and sat down.

John Bosanquet, representing the prosecution lawyers, now rose to address the bench. "Your Lordships," he said smoothly, almost apologetically, "I will not need to occupy the attention of the court for long. All I need to say is that during the prisoner's trial the prosecution followed exactly the same form that has been pursued in similar cases ever since I have had the honour of assisting the Bank of England. The prosecution has always been founded on the utterance of a forged deed, with intent to defraud the Governor and Company of the Bank of England and other parties who might be interested in the deed. I am at a loss to see how it can be contended that a power of attorney – regularly signed, sealed and delivered – can be improperly considered as coming within the meaning of a deed as intended in the Act passed in the fourth year of George the Second." Bosanquet looked up at the judges. "Your Lordships know full well the pains that were taken, and what patient attention the case received from the learned judges, but, after all, the unfortunate person underwent the sentence of the law."

Alley once more took to his feet, but with rather less energy than before. "All I wish to say, Your Lordships, is that I am convinced that the observations of my learned friend on the other side will carry no weight with you. The court will be bound by the law of the case, without regard to the manner in which its decision might affect the prisoner." He sat, but I could see from the slump of his shoulders that he no longer expected to win this argument.

The two judges had a whispered conference before Garrow made a few notes and then looked up and started to speak. "I am not able to satisfy my mind that I can entertain the slightest doubt with respect to the question that has been raised." He shook his head sorrowfully. "If I entertained the opinion that the judgment of death ought not to be pronounced upon the unfortunate gentleman at the bar, I would hasten to declare that opinion, if only in order to show the prisoner some sympathy. However, I owe it to my own feelings, and to a consideration of the awful situation of the prisoner, not to state that I entertain doubts when I entertain none." The judge looked directly at Fauntleroy. "I have looked to the Act of Parliament and have found that the statute mentions the word 'deed' without any qualification. There is no exception in favour of a power of attorney." He cleared his throat. "The awful period has arrived when the unhappy person at the bar is called upon to declare whether he has anything to say why the court should not pass judgment on him to die."

Harmer nodded at Fauntleroy, who stood up slowly and took from his pocket a written statement. He unfolded it carefully, put on his spectacles and started to read. "My Lords, I am well aware that no emergencies, however pressing, that no embarrassments, however great, can be listened to as an excuse for the offence of which I have been found guilty. But I trust that it may be considered as some palliation that a desire to preserve myself and others from bankruptcy, and not personal aggrandisement or selfish gratification, urged and impelled me to the acts I have committed. When I first deviated from rectitude, it was owing to an acute, although I admit mistaken, feeling to obtain temporary relief, and not from any deliberate intention to defraud. God knows my heart, and the truth of my present declaration, that I hoped and fully intended to make restitution immediately the expected prosperity of the house would have enabled me. This must appear evident from my having frequently replaced the money withdrawn, and the bank books will prove that many of the sums mentioned in the document written in 1816 have since been reinvested by me to the credit of the parties.

"Much has been made of my keeping a careful record of these transactions, and the inference has been that I prepared it in contemplation of flight. This is not the case. The only object and intention of that paper was that should I die before repaying the whole of the money, I would absolve everyone beside myself from suspicion."

Garrow wrote for a moment and then motioned the banker to continue.

"Unfortunately for me," said Fauntleroy with a sigh, "a succession of adverse events, which I could neither avert nor control, led from one false step to another until the affairs of the house became so involved that extrication was impossible. For me, fallen and degraded as I am, this life has no allurements, and a momentary pang will at once put an end to my mental agonies. But, my Lords, I have numerous relations, amongst them my dear and venerable mother. For their sakes, I supplicate that I may not be doomed to suffer a violent and ignominious death.

"If crimes can be atoned by suffering, my offences have long been expiated by years of anxious terror and agonising apprehension." I thought back to the haunted and trembling man I had arrested. "And if the anguish of mind I have endured for the last sixteen years of my life could be made known to my most gracious Sovereign, I venture to hope that His Majesty's benevolent and feeling heart would be touched with compassion for my situation, and that I should not be considered an object wholly undeserving of the royal clemency." I recognised the form of words always used in these situations – Harmer must have written this part for him. "May I therefore presume to solicit Your Lordships' humane interposition, to communicate for His Majesty's merciful consideration the circumstances to which I have alluded, and – on behalf of my dearest relations – I supplicate that the punishment of death may be remitted." Fauntleroy folded the paper and put it back into his pocket along with his spectacles.

The banker was then beckoned down from the dock by the clerk and directed to stand in front of it, facing the bench, where he was joined by eleven other men and two women, all of whom had been found guilty of capital offences during the Sessions and had been waiting at the back of the courtroom during the motion and Fauntleroy's petition.

The recorder Knowlys addressed them as a group. "You have been severally convicted by a jury of your fellow countrymen. Bound by their oath they have felt it their duty to consign you to that fate which the law pronounces as a punishment of your crimes. I hope that there is none of you who doubts the justice of that verdict." Knowlys paused and let his gaze range across the group. "None of you is at an age approaching the natural term of your life. All of you are in the full vigour of your body and understanding, yet to this you are reduced by the violation of the laws of God and man. Had these laws been preserved, instead of standing here in this situation, so distressing to everyone who beholds you, you might

have lived in a state of respectability, a comfort to yourself and your friends, instead of an example to those who
shall hear of your fate."

One of the women gave a small cry and seemed about
to faint, and Fauntleroy and the man on the other side of
her held her up between them. Knowlys continued regardless. "Some of you may entertain the idea that mercy
will be extended to you. However, the crimes of some of
you are of a very aggravated character. The forger," and
here he turned his eyes to Fauntleroy, "whose crime
might involve even the richest in irretrievable ruin; the
midnight burglar," he stared at a man standing behind the
banker, "who carried away the property, perhaps the little
all they had, of the inhabitants whose house he entered;
the unfeeling robber," this the man helping Fauntleroy to
support the fainting woman, "who not only takes away
the property but leaves his victim with scarcely any remains of life – these will do well to prepare for death, for
these are crimes to which mercy is seldom extended."

I glanced at Harmer, who made no reaction. No doubt
he had heard the theatricals of the recorder on many such
occasions.

Knowlys pressed on. "It is the duty of you all to look
forward and prepare for your latter end, and to lose not a
moment in making ready for the worst. Of this, however,
you may be assured: whatever favourable circumstances

may appear in any of your cases, they will not be withheld from the consideration of the King.

"Nothing remains for me now but to pass the last sentence of the law, which is that you and each of you be severally conveyed from the bar to the gaol from which you came, and thence to the place of execution, and there hanged by the neck until you are dead, and may God Almighty have mercy on your souls."

"Amen," replied the clerk as the woman beside Fauntleroy finally slipped silently to the floor.

# CHAPTER TWENTY-TWO

# The mad Italian

## THURSDAY 4TH NOVEMBER 1824

From the exasperated look on the mayor's face, I could tell that his visitor had been entertaining him in his Mansion House office for some time.

"Ah, Constable Plank," said Mr Waithman with relief, waving me into the room, "thank you for responding so promptly to my message. Now, Signor Angelini, if you will not listen to me, perhaps you will believe this police constable – he was present throughout Mr Fauntleroy's trial and sentencing two days ago."

Angelini: the name sounded familiar, and I was sure I knew the face too. Of course: Edmund Angelini had been at Great Marlborough Street only a few days before, taken before the magistrates after a fracas with the Austrian ambassador concerning a passport. Something and nothing, and he was bound over to keep the peace. But Mr Angelini, an Italian teacher of languages, was quite a character. He did not make any sign of recognising me, but, as I have often noted, people rarely remember specific police officers.

"Constable Plank," continued Waithman, handing me a piece of paper and retreating behind his desk, "Signor Angelini has come to me with a rather unusual petition, and I have tried to explain to him that with regret – a regret that grows by the minute – we cannot accede to his request."

I read the petition, which was written with extravagant flourishes and much heavy emphasis on certain words. "My Lord," it said, "He who has violated the law ought to perish by the sword of justice – Mr Fauntleroy ought to perish by the sword of justice. If, however, another take his place, I think *justice ought to be satisfied*. Now I *devote* myself for Mr Fauntleroy – now I take upon myself his crime and *wish to die to save him*." I looked at Angelini, who was standing with his hands clasped, watching me intently, and then at Waithman, who simply raised his eyebrows. "He is a father, he is a citizen. His life is useful; mine is *a burden to the world*. I am in good health; my mental faculties are unimpaired. I do not ask this in order to get my action spoken of, but I apply for it as a *great favour.* Your obedient servant, Edmund Angelini of Venezia." The address below his signature was in Somerstown, just north of Newgate.

"I have tried to make it clear to Signor Angelini that this is not how the law works," said Waithman, "and that he, as an educated man, should understand that." Angelini opened his mouth to speak, but the mayor quickly continued. "It is contrary to justice that the life of an innocent man should be taken in place of that of a guilty one."

"But sirs," said Angelini passionately, "we have the best of all examples of just this. Look to your Bible, sirs! As all believers know, our Saviour died as an atonement for the sins of others. I am of sound faculties, so why should I not be permitted to imitate that grand example?"

Waithman looked pleadingly at me.

"Signor Angelini," I said as gently as I could, "your sentiment does you credit. What has Mr Fauntleroy done to inspire such loyalty and generosity?"

"I do not know Mr Fauntleroy, but it is wrong that such a man should die for such an error. If blood is needed, let it be mine – let it be that of unworthy Angelini."

I had seen undeserved devotion before; a woman knocked black and blue by her husband will often defend his right to use her as a punching bag. But to my mind, for one man to offer to die in place of another to whom he has no connection suggests either that there is indeed a connection and it is being hidden, or that the offer is made in madness. And I could not find out which, standing in front of the mayor.

"Signor Angelini," I said, taking his elbow, "as you have heard, the Lord Mayor cannot grant this petition. But if you come with me, we can look further into the matter, and perhaps find another way in which you can help the cause of Mr Fauntleroy." I steered him firmly towards the door. He came meekly enough, but as soon as we got outside he bolted off down Poultry. I considered chasing him but decided against it, presuming that the madman had thought better of his offer.

# CHAPTER TWENTY-THREE

# Petitions and appeals

## WEDNESDAY 10TH NOVEMBER 1824

I lifted the muslin cover on the pot and inhaled deeply. "Not my favourite pigeon pie?"

"What else?" said Martha. She squeezed my shoulder as she laid my plate in front of me. "Your mind is elsewhere tonight, Sam – tell me." Better than a bloodhound, my Martha, at rooting out hidden things. But she was right: I couldn't stop thinking about the Fauntleroy case. Mind you, it was hard to avoid: every newspaper and magazine was full of it, and the taverns and coffeehouses hummed with chatter about the banker and his fate. There were even rumours that the outcry would force the government to change the law on forgery. But before that we had to get through the next few days, and Mr Harmer had explained to me what would be happening.

"So last week Mr Fauntleroy's lawyers tried to convince the judge that the trial had been flawed?" prompted Martha, blowing on her forkful of pie.

"Mmm," I agreed, "and they failed. But Mr Harmer seems to think that the argument still has merit, and that continuing to question the conduct of the trial will shake the public's faith in its verdict. So he is going to ask to be allowed to present another motion in arrest of judgment – that's what they call it – but this time to the Twelve Judges of England."

"They sound important."

"Aye; they're the most senior and learned judges in the land, and the most vexatious cases are sent to them for consideration. Harmer will make an application to the Home Secretary, and if Mr Peel approves, the argument will be put to the Twelve."

"When?" asked Martha.

"That's something of a problem. They do not meet that often, so it cannot be until the twenty-third of the month – which leaves Fauntleroy in Newgate for another fortnight at least." I held out my plate for another slice of pie. "And so to distract him, Mr Harmer has advised Fauntleroy to use the time until then to prepare for an appeal to the King."

"The King!" Martha bobbed a curtsey as she leaned over the table to hand me the gravy.

"Indeed: if he is so minded, Prinny can grant the royal clemency – and send Fauntleroy to gaol rather than the scaffold, or even pardon him completely. So Fauntleroy and his brother – you remember me mentioning him, the lawyer – have already started gathering signatures to their petition."

"Will it work?" asked Martha – always quick to get to the point of a thing.

I shrugged. "I doubt a pardon would be considered suitable; after all, the man has admitted defrauding his customers. But hard labour rather than hanging, and with public opinion turning against the noose…"

"And you, Sam," said Martha, looking directly at me. "You have spent many hours in his company. Does Mr Fauntleroy strike you as a man deserving of clemency?"

And just then, I realised that I didn't know. Not for the first time, I was very glad that my job was to catch miscreants, and not to judge them.

Not all of my time was spent on the Fauntleroy case, of course, but I felt that Mr Conant was encouraging me to pursue our enquiries by pushing fewer other duties in my direction. To a certain extent my task was made easier by the constant reporting and dissection of the case; it seemed that everyone had an opinion. It didn't hurt Fauntleroy that Mr Harmer himself owned the *Weekly*

*Dispatch*, and every time a salvo against the banker appeared in, say, *The Times*, a quick rebuttal would soon be published in the *Dispatch*. Certain papers kept a running tally of the number of signatures on the petition for royal clemency, and the total soon reached three thousand.

Among the early subscribers to the petition was the clergyman Charles Bowdler, who had long campaigned against the death penalty for forgery on the grounds that no property is worth a human life. I was just reading his arguments in the most recent *Dispatch* when the office-keeper put his head around the door.

"You've visitors, Sam – a Mrs Fauntleroy and her son."

It was the first time that I had seen Marianne Fauntleroy; she had not been at any of her husband's hearings, or at the trial. She was one of those women who do not age well; there were lines on her porcelain prettiness, and a disappointed sourness to her expression. But she held herself proudly, and settled graciously into the chair that I indicated. Her son stood behind her with his hand on her shoulder; he had his father's colouring and delicate features, and perhaps unsurprisingly looked more care-worn than his fifteen years should have allowed.

"Mrs Fauntleroy," I said, "how may I help you?"

"I have been reading of my husband's ordeal in the newspapers." Her voice was faint and she chose her words precisely, suggesting someone who spends more time listening than speaking. "As you will have gathered, my husband and I no longer share a home."

I nodded; the details of the banker's private life had been chewed over many times in the press.

She smoothed down her skirt and continued. "Henry has many failings, that I do not doubt. But as a provider, he has never stinted: he has met all of his financial responsibilities to me and to our son." She reached up and placed her hand over that of the boy. "Today I am taking Henry to see his father in Newgate. My brother-in-law John is waiting for us outside and will accompany us. It was he who suggested that I should come to you with my enquiry."

"Madam, I would advise against your going to Newgate…"

She held up her hand. "I am well aware of the conditions that I will encounter – the press is at least helpful in that regard. But it is important that Henry should speak with his father and know that he is not a wicked man. A foolish man, perhaps, and certainly one who has made some grave mistakes, but not a wicked man."

"And how may I be of assistance, Mrs Fauntleroy? Do you wish me to accompany you to Newgate?"

She shook her head, and addressed her son without taking her eyes off my face. "Henry, go and wait with your uncle while I speak with the constable."

Once the boy had left, Mrs Fauntleroy leaned towards me and spoke in an urgent tone. "As I explained, over the years my husband has paid me an annual allowance, and school fees and other incidentals. If it turns out that the money was not his to give, do I need to repay it? It is spent, but I have assets that I could sell."

I have to say that Mrs Fauntleroy rose enormously in my estimation. That she should think through the implications of her husband's actions, and that she should wish to make reparation to his victims, made me think that perhaps his hasty choice of wife had been a wiser decision than he had realised – or indeed deserved. I had to admit that I did not know the answer to her question, and promised to address it to Mr Harmer on her behalf. She thanked me, and left. I still wonder what she and her silent son thought of Newgate.

"Quite a woman, Marianne Fauntleroy," said Harmer as we strode along Holborn later that day and I told him of my visitor. I had quickly learned that the best time to catch the lawyer and hold his attention was as he walked between his chambers and his clients in Newgate. "I can't see any of the creditors pursuing her for the money, so you can reassure her on that matter."

"I shall, with great pleasure," I replied.

"It is something of a coincidence that you should meet Mrs Fauntleroy today," said Harmer. "Here," he dug into his satchel as he walked, "look at this." He handed me a paper. "This was delivered to the Home Office yesterday; one of the clerks there was persuaded to make me a copy." He winked at me.

We stopped for a moment so that I could read the paper without coming to grief. "To His Most Excellent Majesty King George the Fourth: The very humble petition of Marianne Fauntleroy." I looked up at Harmer in astonishment. He indicated that I should continue reading. "Forgive, O most gracious Sire, a wretched and distracted woman, for presuming to approach your royal person to supplicate for mercy to be extended to the unfortunate Henry Fauntleroy. Let not, I beseech you, the dreadful punishment of an ignominious death be inflicted on the husband of your supplicant – the father of her child. But spare, O mercifully spare, the father's life, that disgrace may not be entailed on his innocent offspring, and overwhelming misery inflicted on your petitioner.

"Your petitioner most respectfully assures Your Majesty that the royal clemency cannot be afforded to a more deserving object than her unhappy husband; he possesses a most sympathetic and feeling heart, and an honourable and generous mind. Do not, therefore, most excellent Sovereign, allow the full rigour of the law to be put in force, but temper justice with the divine attribute mercy, and leave the all-great and bountiful Creator to take away that life which he alone can give.

"And your humble petitioner, with her dear and innocent child, will continually offer up their grateful prayers for every blessing and happiness to attend Your Majesty, for ever and ever."

I handed the paper back to Harmer, who stuffed it into his satchel and started walking again.

"Now that's what I call a forgiving woman!" he said. "And her petition will help ours, I feel sure. But well over half of those sentenced to death submit petitions, so we need to do all we can to make sure that ours stands out when Peel comes to read it."

"Surely he doesn't read them himself."

"Ah, well, there you are wrong, constable," said Harmer, flinging out his arm to stop me walking in front of a hackney and then ushering me across the road once it had passed. "Our Mr Peel has a reputation for being the most conscientious Home Secretary in years. And in particular he prides himself on reading each and every petition. So we need to make sure that ours catches his eye – and having thousands of signatures is a good way to do that. We're making it even more conspicuous by delivering it to the Home Office in bundles, as though we can't keep up with it all. By the way, you'll never guess who called in just this morning to add his name. William Marsh."

"The senior partner at Fauntleroy's bank?"

"The very same. Strange old bird. Didn't say much; just signed, and observed that he'd had an excellent chop for breakfast. So now we have all of the bank's partners signed up, which shows that they're standing by their man and don't think that he was trying to cheat them."

"Don't they?" I asked.

"Not in public at least, and that's what counts. If the fellow's own partners, who are perhaps the most affected by his actions, don't think he's a crook, then it makes it all the harder to send him to the hangman. And an execution, once stayed, is much easier to halt altogether: haste is very much our enemy. We need people to question the process and demand delay, and public support seems to be with us. Have you seen this?" He stopped abruptly and dipped into his satchel again, pulling out a newspaper which he handed to me. "There: I've circled it to show to Mr Fauntleroy."

It was that day's edition of the *Morning Chronicle*, a letter sent in by "An Observer": "Sir – From the tone of this unfortunate gentleman's defence at his trial, and the peculiar nature of the transactions which formed the subject of his guilt, insinuations are now scattering about. Commiseration for his dreadful fate seems almost to give the force of demonstration to what is only vague assertion and random suspicion. As an impartial observer, I cannot help submitting whether the most ordinary rules of justice do not require us to pause until we hear both sides, and have proofs, authenticated and indubitable proofs, before us." I looked closely at Harmer as I handed the newspaper back to him. "Well-reasoned," I said. "Almost as though a lawyer had written it."

We had reached the steps of Newgate. "The very idea, constable," said Harmer with a smile as he shook my hand in farewell. "The very idea."

# CHAPTER TWENTY-FOUR

# The plea for clemency

## MONDAY 22ND NOVEMBER 1824

Some days later I was heading back to Great Marlborough Street in the late afternoon when someone hailed me from across the street – it was Mr Harmer.

"Constable Plank, will you join me for a drink? I feel in need of some refreshment – the stench of Newgate sticks in the throat."

Once we were settled with our ale and the lawyer had taken a long restorative draught of his, I asked how Fauntleroy's petition was progressing.

"Excellent, excellent. The Twelve Judges hear the case tomorrow, so I delivered the final signatures to the Home

Office yesterday evening – into the hand of Mr Peel himself."

"Tell me, Mr Harmer, do you think the petition will help?"

Harmer paused before answering. "The charge against my client is very serious, there is no denying that. But Peel would not have received me personally if he was not taking a particular interest in this case. And he promised to lay the petition before the King-in-Council, should the Twelve Judges dismiss our appeal. I do not think he would take up His Majesty's time with a hopeless cause. And his clerk hinted as he saw me out that Peel has even discussed the case with Lord Liverpool."

"Well, if the Prime Minister has become involved..."

"He can hardly ignore it, given the size of the thing."

"How many signatures are there now?"

"About twenty-five thousand," said Harmer, draining his tankard.

I was amazed. "But that's one for every five people living in London!"

"Including this rather heartfelt one," said Harmer, reaching into his satchel for a newspaper. "There," he tapped on the page, "read that letter."

I turned the paper to the window to catch the light. "Sir – Having read about the petition respecting Fauntleroy's case, I never rested until my signature was attached to it, although I am actually a sufferer to a large amount

from this culprit's fraudulent conduct." I raised my eyebrows at Harmer, who was looking disappointedly into
his empty tankard, and then continued reading. "God
forbid, however, that he should be prosecuted to death,
for it is full time that our too sanguinary code should be
whitewashed by the merciful hands of the Sovereign.
Were Fauntleroy alone to suffer, there might be a shadow
of apology for excluding him from the benefit of pending
ameliorations of our laws, but his near relatives, affec-
tionate friends, and particularly his most interesting boy
will probably live long enough to see the expected change
from cruelty to mercy. This really is torturing through
life an innocent child for the venial trespasses of a guilty
parent – for, after all, what is property when put in competition with that breath which God alone can give and,
when once taken away, no mortal on earth can restore?
Oh that the small still voice of reason, which runs
through the milk of human nature in the breast of one
who is more of a sinner than a saint, could yet arrest the
vindictive arm of English justice ere it be too late, then
indeed I should feel happy in so far doing my duty for the
glory of my country, my benevolent faith and the lasting
honour of the reigning Monarch and his illustrious race.
From A Man." I looked up questioningly at Harmer.

"No, not this time!" he laughed. "The language is a bit
flowery for me. A poet, perhaps – or a clergyman. No

matter: he is on our side. And now I must be away to my chambers."

The next evening I was once again in Wontner's office in Newgate; it had become a habit of mine to call in when passing. Besides, I knew that the Twelve Judges had met that afternoon and I hoped to glean the latest news. And indeed, not long after my arrival there was a knock at the door and in came Mr Harmer and Mr Forbes. Harmer dropped into a chair and said two words only. "An adjournment."

"An adjournment!" echoed Wontner. "On what grounds?"

Harmer shrugged. "Hard to say. Mr Brodrick put the case to the Twelve Judges this afternoon, elaborating on the legal point he made last time – about whether a power of attorney counts as a deed for the purposes of forgery." Wontner and I nodded. "Once Brodrick had put his case, the Twelve Judges withdrew to consider, and then returned to say that they were calling for an adjournment until tomorrow."

"But why?" I asked. I had thought that such was their learning and seniority that their decision would be instant and binding.

"My guess," suggested Harmer, "would be that they wish to consult the legislation themselves, and see if there are any relevant precedents – other findings on this matter to which they can refer."

"Is that a good sign? Or a bad?" I wondered aloud.

"My dear constable," said Harmer, shaking his head, "trying to guess the minds of the Twelve Judges is a sure route to madness – better men than you and I have tried and failed. But I think it hopeful that they did not dismiss the argument out of hand. Distressing though it is for all of us, we must wait until tomorrow." He rose wearily from his chair. "And now you will excuse me, as I must convey this latest news to Mr Fauntleroy."

But it was a false dawn of hope for both Harmer and his client, and the appeal was dismissed by the Twelve Judges the very next day. So that was the second of Harmer's three weapons discharged to no effect, and now everything rested on the appeal for royal clemency.

Harmer explained the process to us all as we gathered once again in Fauntleroy's cell that Wednesday evening. The recorder Mr Knowlys and the home secretary Mr Peel would call on the King and his privy council, who were meeting at Carlton House after lunch on the morrow, where Knowlys would present a list of those sentenced to death at the last Sessions. Peel would highlight the ones for which petitions had been received, make short comments on their merits or otherwise, and then the King would decide where to grant clemency.

The next day, Thursday the twenty-fifth of November, Wontner and I waited in his office, trying to distract ourselves. He read papers and attended to business, while I looked back through my notebook, trying to piece together a clearer picture of this banker who troubled me so.

Shortly after three o'clock, there was a quiet knock at the door. "Come in!" called Wontner, and the Reverend Cotton entered the office. So cast down was his demeanour that there was no need for him to explain; he simply shook his head. Wontner sighed deeply and pushed himself up from his seat.

"Come, constable – we must tell Mr Fauntleroy."

When we arrived at his cell, I was surprised to see Fauntleroy on his knees at prayer – but then men sensing their mortality do often conceive a renewed interest in their souls. He scrambled to his feet. Harmer was sitting in the armchair, papers spread out on the floor before him. The cell felt suddenly crowded, with the banker and his lawyer, the keeper and me, Cotton and the pale young man who had accompanied him.

"Mr Fauntleroy," began Cotton, "Mr Denning and I have come from the recorder – Mr Denning is his clerk. We have here the report from the recorder regarding the outcome of the meeting of the King-in-Council." Cotton held out his hand, and Denning passed him a sheet of paper, which Cotton in turn passed to Fauntleroy. I caught sight of a black seal. "The report is fatal to you, and I trust and believe that you are prepared. As you see, the date of your execution has been set for the thirtieth of November – five days hence."

Fauntleroy nodded wordlessly.

Cotton continued. "I shall call on the other prisoners mentioned in the recorder's report, and then return to you, and perhaps we shall pray together."

"The others," said Fauntleroy. "Ah yes. That poor woman. But I hope that I am to suffer alone – that no other poor creature is to go out of the world at the same time?"

"That is so," confirmed Denning. "The other petitions placed before the King were granted clemency."

"All of them?" asked Harmer sharply. "All admitted to clemency except ours?"

Mr Denning nodded nervously.

"Any reasons given?"

Mr Denning shook his head, and started to back towards the door.

Harmer frowned. "Someone has had a hand in this. Someone able to influence the King. Otherwise how could he ignore a petition of thirty thousand signatures, concerning a crime that he himself has declared should not involve the scaffold, while granting clemency to all and sundry? Constable Plank, I have need of your nose for information."

After dinner that evening, Martha and I sat by the fire, she darning a stocking and me just staring into the flames. She reached across and patted my hand.

"Come now, Sam – he is not the first man you have known condemned to hang." I said nothing, for of course she was right. "And it is not as though his conviction is unjust, is it? He has admitted the crime, after all. Hmm?" I nodded. "So what is it that worries you?"

I frowned as I tried to explain – as much to myself as to her. "There's just something not quite right about it all. Firstly, yes, he has admitted the forgery, and yes, the penalty is death – but most people of standing and influence think that it should not be. And many of those very people have been involved in this case, not least the King himself. Secondly, at the trial there was a procession of the great and the good, speaking on Fauntleroy's behalf, and so the judges and jury had every excuse to show leniency, and yet they did not. Why not?"

Martha bit off the thread she was using. "Didn't you say that those who run the Bank of England were determined to see him punished severely? That they feared that if he got away with it, others would follow?"

"Yes, there is that. But I doubt that even the governor of the Bank of England could dissuade the King from granting clemency, if he were minded to grant it. So why wasn't he? He granted it to every other criminal condemned alongside Fauntleroy, but not to him, even though thirty thousand petitioners called for it – why not?"

Martha shook her head. "I'm not sure you'll get anywhere trying to guess Prinny's motives."

"But what really troubles me," and as I said it I suddenly knew. "What really troubles me is his reaction."

"The King's?"

"No, no – Fauntleroy's. When Wontner and I went with the recorder's clerk to tell Fauntleroy that the clemency had not been granted, he was, well, calm. He didn't shout or protest, or even question the decision. He simply asked whether the others sentenced alongside him had been spared, and then carried on as before."

"Maybe he's the sort to keep it all inside," suggested Martha.

I shook my head. "No – I've seen him cry out in desperation in court, and fall to his knees weeping in his cell. But not this time. And this is when you might expect it – when all hope is gone. So what has changed between those previous outbursts, and now?"

# CHAPTER TWENTY-FIVE

# At the Home Office

## FRIDAY 26TH NOVEMBER 1824

The next morning I set off for the Home Office. Something significant had altered between Fauntleroy agreeing to petition for clemency and the outcome of that petition – and so the petition itself seemed a good place to start. I explained my business to the guard at the entrance, and he pointed me in the direction of the office where petitions are received and prepared for the attention of the Home Secretary. I looked through the half-frosted door, and counted four clerks: three in their middle years and one more junior. I knocked and went in. The junior clerk came across to me, rubbing ineffectually at an ink smudge on his cuff.

"I am Constable Samuel Plank, conducting enquiries on behalf of James Harmer Esquire, solicitor." One of the older clerks, who had looked up at my arrival, turned back to his work – nothing to interest him here, which was just as I had hoped. "So as not to disturb these other gentlemen, perhaps you could step outside for a moment." I held the door open for the clerk. Once outside the room, away from curious ears, I continued. "I am interested in petitions that have been submitted concerning Mr Henry Fauntleroy. Are you familiar with his case?"

The young man rolled his eyes. "Familiar? It's all I've been doing for days now, lugging his papers around. No sooner do I get one bundle sorted out than another arrives – we've had to store them in a cupboard under the stairs. Are you here to take it all away? Is it done with now?"

I shook my head. "Not quite yet, no. But tell me, that is all one petition, is it not?" He nodded. "And you have had others for the same man, I believe? One from his wife?"

The clerk held up a hand and started ticking off on his fingers. "We've had petitions from his wife, his friends, his creditors – if you can believe that."

"His creditors?" I asked. "Why would they want him reprieved? Is it possible for me to see their petition?" The clerk hesitated and looked over his shoulder. I reached into my breast pocket and casually adjusted the contents so that the corner of a pound note peeped out. The clerk's eyes followed my hand. The lure of an extra week's wages was usually irresistible.

"Wait here," he said, indicating a bench by the wall. He went back into his office, and came out a few minutes later with a folder of papers. He sat next to me, glanced up and down the corridor, and then opened the folder on his lap. "Here – but read it quickly," he said, sliding it towards me.

"To the King's Most Excellent Majesty in Council," I read. "The humble petition of the undersigned creditors of William Marsh, Josias Henry Stracey, George Edward Graham and Henry Fauntleroy, late carrying on business as bankers in Berners Street, in the County of Middlesex, Bankrupts, sheweth -

"That your petitioners, on their own account, and on behalf of other creditors of the late banking house of Marsh and Company, are very importantly interested in obtaining a full disclosure and discovery of all the dealings and transactions of the said house during the last fifteen years and upwards.

"That your petitioners are informed, and believe, that the said Henry Fauntleroy, who has been convicted for uttering a false instrument, has since the year 1807 had the principal management and conduct of the affairs of the said banking house, and is alone able to furnish the information which must be required to elucidate the nature of the transactions of the said house in which your petitioners are interested. A full and correct statement of the facts, and the course of the various transactions, we believe can only be obtained from the said Henry Fauntleroy, who, we have been informed, will be ready to give all information in his power.

"That if the said Henry Fauntleroy should suffer death before the legal determination of the questions above alluded to can be obtained, great injury may be sustained by your petitioners and other creditors of the said bankrupts' estate, who are very numerous.

"Your petitioners, the said creditors, therefore humbly presume to pray that His Majesty may be pleased to commute the sentence of death passed upon the said Henry Fauntleroy, or that he may be respited until a sufficient period of time shall have elapsed for obtaining the disclosure and discoveries above-mentioned. And your petitioners, as in duty bound, will ever pray."

So the creditors wanted Fauntleroy kept alive long enough for them to find out what he had done with their money – that at least made sense. But it did not explain why the banker was so sanguine about the failure of the petition. Surely he did not so dread giving his creditors the information they sought that he would rather face the noose?

The clerk went to close the folder, and as he did so a single sheet of paper fell from it. I reached down to retrieve it, and to my astonishment I saw on it a signature that I knew only too well: that of Henry Fauntleroy. Con-

demned prisoners are not permitted to petition for clemency on their own behalf, so what could it be? The clerk
reached to take the paper from me, but I held up my hand
to stay him.

"To the King's Most Excellent Majesty in Council," I
read. "Several petitions have been submitted concerning
my lamentable situation. Those who are assembling,
promoting and subscribing to these petitions mean well,
and I do not wish to appear ungrateful by discouraging
their efforts. But nor do I wish to mislead His Majesty as
to my own very definite wishes in this matter.

"I am guilty of forgery, and of uttering a forged instrument. The penalty for such offences – which I knew full
well before embarking on them – is death. Many men
consider this the most terrible of punishments, but for
me, even more terrible would be the loss of my honour
and my reputation. Should His Majesty grant me the
royal clemency, I will endure the most severe punishment
for the rest of my life, knowing that the name of Fauntleroy will be forever associated with a failed bank.

"For me, true clemency will take the form of permitting the sentence of the court to be carried out, thus ending my torment. Regardless of the fine words and
laudable sentiments of others, please assure His Majesty
that this humble petitioner, the one whom this matter
most closely concerns, has no wish to live in disgrace, but
wishes only to pay the price that the law and the court

have judged appropriate." The signature was dated the nineteenth of November 1824 – even before the meeting of the Twelve Judges. It seemed that, regardless of the efforts being made on his behalf by so many, the banker was determined to hang, and moreover had made every effort to let Mr Peel and even the King know his wishes. I handed the paper back to the clerk, with the pound note hidden beneath it.

# CHAPTER TWENTY-SIX

# Fire and brimstone

SUNDAY 28TH NOVEMBER 1824

Martha had tried to dissuade me from going, but it had seemed a small enough gesture to make, when Wontner had suggested it: to attend chapel with Fauntleroy. The keeper and I walked as so often before to the banker's cell, but this time through strangely quiet passageways.

"It's always like this, the Sunday before an execution," observed Wontner. "The prisoners are like animals: they sense despair, and it unnerves them."

We reached the cell to find Fauntleroy and Harmer waiting for us and we set off at once. The four of us, accompanied by two guards, skirted the men's quadrangle and headed for the chapel.

"I understand that Mr Cotton is in fine voice today; one of my junior keepers heard him doing vocal exercises after breakfast," said Wontner conversationally. "You know, Mr Fauntleroy," he stopped and laid a hand on the banker's arm, "you mustn't be alarmed by Cotton's sermon. He's very fire and brimstone – a bit too much for my taste, frankly. I think he harrows the prisoners unnecessarily, and I've said as much to my masters. He'll thunder and roar today, particularly as he has an audience."

"An audience?" asked Fauntleroy.

"Aye. I'm sorry to say that several people of a morbid turn of mind have obtained tickets to attend the service – you're quite an attraction, I'm afraid. You'll have to sit in the condemned pew, but you'll not be alone. Mr Forbes and Mr Wadd have asked to be permitted to sit with you."

Reverend Cotton, his white gown billowing around him, gripped the pulpit with both hands. "On particular occasions in the history of society," he declaimed, "crimes have been brought to light of a nature so peculiar and of an extent so alarming as to call for the severest punishment the laws can inflict. Many offenders have been situated similarly to the unhappy man before us now," and here Cotton paused and stared meaningfully at Fauntleroy, who dropped his gaze and clutched his prayer-book. On either side of him sat the surgeon Wadd and the lawyer Forbes, looking straight ahead at the preacher, and with their shoulders touching Fauntleroy as though to prop him upright. "But no case for many years has excited a deeper public interest or a more considerable portion of public sympathy. Petition followed petition to the throne. But our erring brother's offence is of great magnitude, and one of the most dangerous in a commercial country. In extent it is perhaps unparalleled in the history of such crimes."

Cotton continued in this vein for some minutes. "Oh my dear brother," he dropped his voice to a theatrical whisper and looked at the banker, "oh my dear brother, believe in the Lord Jesus Christ and thou shalt be saved. Many of your sins are known only to God and to your own heart, and none of them which is unrepented can be forgiven. It is your duty to do all in your power to make honourable amends to the parties who have been injured by you, and may God Almighty impart to you the desire to give this proof of your repentance."

# CHAPTER TWENTY-SEVEN

# Forgive thee thine offences

## TUESDAY 30<sup>TH</sup> NOVEMBER 1824

It was a cold day with a light drizzle, but thankfully the high winds of the previous week had died down. I tried not to attend executions; of course I had seen a few, but I knew only too well how the mood of a crowd could change. And I have never understood how the death of a fellow human being can be a source of entertainment. But I had promised Mr Wontner that I would accompany the banker to the scaffold; the keeper was of the view that the last faces a man sees in this life should be familiar ones, not a pack of bloodthirsty strangers. From her reassuring squeeze of my hand and the warmth of her kiss on my cheek as I left home, I could tell that Martha sensed my unease.

What I had been unable to share, even with her, was the source of that unease. It was not simply my distaste for executions, nor my belief that no financial crime, no matter how extensive, should end on the scaffold. And to be sure, if my involvement with this case had convinced me of anything, it was that. No, it was my policeman's instinct that I had missed something.

As I arrived at the stone steps of Newgate, I saw two turnkeys tussling with a man at the door. As he tried to get past them, he caught sight of me and called out. "Constable Plank! It is I, Edmund Angelini." He addressed the turnkeys. "This police officer will vouch for me. I am here today to take the place of Mr Fauntleroy on the scaffold – Constable Plank, you know that I have permission from the Lord Mayor!"

The two turnkeys looked at me, but did not release their hold on the Italian. "He wants to be taken to the ordinary, to receive the sacrament," explained one of them.

I indicated to them to let him go and then took hold myself of Angelini's shoulders to keep him still. "Signor," I said in a low tone that I often use to quieten the agitated, "Signor, you will remember that the Lord Mayor told you some weeks ago that what you request is impossible. You cannot hang for another man's crime." I looked straight into his eyes. "It is not possible, Signor. You must go home now, and let the law take its correct course."

Angelini gazed about him, as though seeing his surroundings for the first time. "Please tell Mr Fauntleroy how sorry I am that I cannot take his place today." He then shook my hand, gave a small bow to the turnkeys, and abruptly left. The turnkeys stared after him, shaking their heads.

I went to Wontner's office just as the clock of St Sepulchre was striking seven. Harmer and the keeper were waiting there for me, and we walked in silence to Fauntleroy's cell. None of us felt like talking. The banker was not alone; sitting quietly in one of the chairs, a prayerbook open in his hands, was a lean, white-haired man whom I did not know. He smiled warmly at us as we entered the cell.

"Mr Benjamin Baker," explained Wontner in a whisper. "Prison visitor. He's been here all night; he does not think a condemned man should be alone in his final hours. Map engraver by profession."

The banker was wearing a freshly-laundered white shirt and stock, black knee-breeches and tailcoat, black silk stockings, and dress shoes. He nodded to acknowledge us, and then knelt carefully on the rug. Baker knelt alongside him and recited quietly, "When thou goest through the waters they shall not overflow thee, and when thou passest through the Valley of the Shadow of Death I will be with thee." The two men prayed silently for some minutes, until Fauntleroy said out loud, "Thy mercy, Lord, is all I ask – Lord, let Thy mercy come."

There were footsteps in the passageway, and John Forbes and William Wadd arrived. Wadd nodded at Wontner, who cleared his throat. "Mr Fauntleroy, sir," he said, "I believe that Mr Cotton is ready to start the service."

The banker stayed on his knees, his eyes closed. Eventually Mr Baker touched his elbow, and they both got to their feet. Suddenly Fauntleroy looked about himself in a panic. "My prayer-book! I must have my prayer-book!"

"Here it is, my friend – here it is." And Mr Baker handed it to him.

We made our way in silent procession to the chamber known as the condemned room. At this early hour the room was only dimly lit by six large windows high in the walls, down which the rain was now making its steady course. A small fire burned in the grate, providing a modicum of warmth. There was a long table in the middle of the room, with a bench on either side of it and three candles spaced along it. A small pulpit stood nearby. Apart from this plain furniture, the room was bare. The Rev-

erend Cotton was standing at the pulpit, and acknowledged our arrival with a slight inclination of his head. We
arranged ourselves around the table, and I noticed that
Mr Baker and Mr Wadd in wordless agreement stood either side of the banker, close enough to touch him.

"We shall sing the hymn that the prisoner has requested," said Cotton. Hymn books were passed among
us, already opened to the correct page, and handed to the
four guards who were also in the room. We started to
sing. "God moves in a mysterious way, His wonders to
perform; He plants His footsteps in the sea, And rides
upon the storm..." I saw the banker wipe away a tear.
"Judge not the Lord by feeble sense, But trust Him for His
grace; Behind a frowning providence, He hides a smiling
face."

At the end of the hymn, Cotton led us in prayer and
then stepped from behind the pulpit and approached the
banker, indicating that he should kneel. Standing before
him, the clergyman asked, "Dost thou believe in God the
Father Almighty, maker of heaven and earth? And in Jesus Christ, His only-begotten Son our Lord? And dost
thou believe in the Holy Ghost, the remission of sins, and
everlasting life after death?"

"I do," whispered Fauntleroy, his head bowed.

"Do you repent you truly of your sins?"

"I do."

"Do you forgive, from the bottom of your heart, all those who have offended you?"

"I do."

"If you have offended others, have you asked their forgiveness, and if you have done them wrong, have you done all you can to make amends?"

Fauntleroy paused and we waited. "I have."

Cotton placed his hand on the banker's head. "Our Lord Jesus Christ, who hath left power to His church to absolve all sinners who truly repent and believe in Him, of His great mercy forgive thee thine offences. And by His authority committed to me, I absolve thee from all thy sins. In the name of the Father, and of the Son, and of the Holy Ghost. Amen."

"Amen," we echoed.

The short service over, we all gathered closer to the fire – the high ceilings and large windows made it a chilly room. A church bell started to toll the hour. Cotton walked towards Fauntleroy and two of the guards came up to the banker, bent his arms behind him and tied them with a thin rope. Wadd stepped forward and embraced Fauntleroy. "God be with you, my friend," he said.

The sheriff, in his black robe and lace collar, had slipped into the room. He approached the banker and bowed. "You are Henry Fauntleroy?" he asked. The banker nodded. "Then it is my unfortunate duty to escort you from this room." The sheriff turned and walked towards the door, and Cotton followed him. Baker and Wontner stood one either side of Fauntleroy and linked their arms through his crooked elbows. The rest of us fell in behind them as they left the room.

The sheriff and the ordinary led us at a measured pace through a long vaulted passage. We turned to the left, through a heavy door held open by a guard, and down a steep stone staircase. We were now in a tunnel, with lamps placed at rare and irregular intervals along the damp curved walls. We walked beneath eight arches, each narrower than the last, so that we were forced to crowd closer together. At the end of the tunnel the floor sloped upwards. We found ourselves in a square courtyard open to the sky, from which the rain fell steadily, and facing a tall gate leading out into the street. Beyond the gate we could hear what sounded like a busy market, with shouts and cries and footsteps and the noises of animals. Cotton stopped and turned to face Fauntleroy, his prayer book open in his hands.

"Man that is born of a woman hath but a short time to live." he read. "He cometh up and is cut down like a flower." The banker's knees buckled; but for the tight grasp of the two men at his side he would have fallen to the ground. "Spare us, Lord most holy, God most mighty, holy and merciful Saviour, Thou most worthy judge eternal, suffer us not, at our last hour, for any pains of death, to fall from Thee." Cotton bowed his head. The gates swung open and I turned my head away from the sudden onslaught of noise and movement.

The roar of the crowd was tremendous. People were jammed into every space: every window was packed with faces, every foothold in every wall had been sequestered, every cart was a stage from which dozens craned and yelled. The sheriff climbed up the steps to the wooden platform of the portable scaffold known as the new drop. Cotton and Baker followed him, with Fauntleroy walking between them. Wontner, Harmer and I waited at the foot of the steps with the guards. As the banker stepped onto the platform, every man in that huge, dense, suffocating throng removed his hat.

The sheriff beckoned the banker forward until he was standing beneath a cross-bar. "Help me!" Fauntleroy breathed. "Help me God!" The hangman placed a hood over Fauntleroy's head and put the noose around his neck, deftly adjusting the knot. I prayed that he had calculated the right length for the rope. I closed my eyes. Beside me, Wontner prayed quietly. The crowd fell silent. With a sharp crack the trapdoor opened.

# CHAPTER TWENTY-EIGHT

# Great Scotland Yard

## 1830 – SIX YEARS LATER

For weeks afterwards, the printers made a fortune from the broadsides they produced about the execution of Henry Fauntleroy. The most popular of these – "An Account of the Trial, Execution and Dying Behaviour of Henry Fauntleroy" – claimed to know the banker's "prison thoughts" the night before his death. And although I know ordinaries often supplemented their income by selling their stories in this way, I did not think that Cotton would have taken such a risk this time. An estimated hundred thousand people had watched Fauntleroy hang, some of them paying as much as twenty shillings to owners of nearby premises for permission to observe from their prime windows. But the broadsides were soon dropped into the gutters, and few people concerned themselves again with Henry Fauntle-roy.

Certainly no gawpers were in attendance when the banker was buried a few days after his execution, early in December of 1824. A biting north-easterly wind blew across Bunhill Fields as I stood at a respectful distance from his family to witness his interment. His sister Elizabeth's sobbing was the only sound apart from the rattling of wind-whipped tree branches; between Elizabeth and John Fauntleroy, their mother stood rigid and dry-eyed. There were no other mourners. The minister was dressed in the plainest of vestments, a pair of worn black boots showing beneath the hem of a cassock made for a shorter man. Four grave-diggers tucked their caps into their pockets and slung the ropes over their shoulders. At a silent signal from one of them, they grasped the ropes, heaved, and positioned the coffin over the waiting grave. The minister nodded and the four men let the ropes play slowly through their hands. The coffin descended into the black earth. The minister picked up a trowel of soil and scattered it into the grave. He made to pass the trowel to John Fauntleroy, who shook his head. Instead, the lawyer – looking paler then ever – turned and escorted his mother and sister from the graveside. As he passed me, he acknowledged me with a nod but did not speak.

Before I left Bunhill Fields, I walked across to the new grave, drawing my coat around me against the wind. A solitary grave-digger had been left to fill in the hole, the others having scurried off with the minister the moment the interment was over. Headstones on either side of Fauntleroy's grave marked the final resting places of his father and brother, and of two little sisters who had died before they left the nursery. So much grief for one family. So much grief.

With Henry Fauntleroy dead, my professional involvement in his case came to an end. Occasionally I would open a newspaper and see an advertisement for a meeting of the bank's creditors, or a plea for information in support of bankruptcy petitions, but the Fauntleroy name faded quickly from view, as the banker himself had wished.

I continued working as a constable for the magistrates in Great Marlborough Street, and when the policing of London was reorganised in the summer of 1829 I was one of the first to transfer to the new Metropolitan Police Force. I could have stayed with the magistrates, but I had a deal of respect for the two new Commissioners of Police, and London had grown so vast and so wild that I agreed with their view that the city was now sorely in need of an integrated police force. With my years of experience, I was quickly put to work training new recruits.

Many of them were hot-headed young ex-soldiers, who needed to learn that our role was not just to arrest criminals, but also to inspire confidence and calm in the people of London by acting as disciplined professionals and not as hired thugs.

I had been with the new force for about a year when I was summoned to Great Scotland Yard. Martha had an inkling that this meeting would be important, and spent the evening before polishing the eight gilt buttons on my blue frock coat to the very highest shine. I arrived early, of course, but was kept waiting for only a few minutes before being called into the office of Richard Mayne, one of the two Commissioners. A lawyer by training, he was much younger than I had expected, although the pressures of the job were already starting to show on his face, and his hair was greying at the temples. He reached across a desk piled high with papers to shake my hand.

"Sergeant Plank, I am delighted to meet you at last. You are one of our most valuable men, I am told." (I report this not to sound boastful, but simply to explain why he made the offer that he then made.) He indicated that I should sit. "As you may be aware, the Metropolitan Police Force has excited a great deal of interest around the world." I knew this to be true; other countries, still labouring with fragmented and corrupt systems of control, were watching our progress carefully. "I have here..." he scrabbled among the papers in front of him, before finding the one he wanted and holding it triumphantly aloft, "a request from Sir George Don." I must have looked nonplussed. "The governor of Gibraltar."

"Gibraltar? Our new colony?" I had read something about it a few weeks before.

"Indeed. And much is changing there at the moment. Sir George is an energetic man, and has grand plans. He is setting up a supreme court, and wishes to have an efficient police force to complement it. I find that I have promised to send him one of my best men to oversee recruitment and training." He paused. "I need a man with experience and good sense, a man without onerous family obligations, an incorruptible and efficient man. And everyone I ask seems to think that you are he, Sergeant Plank."

"South of Spain?" asked Martha that evening. "Isn't that Africa?"

"Not quite," I said, "but not far off – less than ten miles away across the water."

"And what do you know about this Gibraltar, Sam? Is it dangerous?"

"Commissioner Mayne gave me some information passed on to him by the governor Sir George Don – you can read it yourself if you wish. They had a bad bout of yellow fever some years back, but Sir George has spent a fortune on improvements since then: new drains, street lighting, rebuilding the hospital – even a botanic gardens."

"So, Sergeant Samuel Plank, what you're telling me is that you will be strolling around shady gardens with dusky Spanish maidens while I sit at home darning your socks."

"That's about the size of it, Mrs Martha Plank." I winked at her. "Does that mean that you think I should go?"

She put down the petticoat she was trimming and looked across at me with softness in her eyes. "Sam, you're fifty years old. How many more adventures are you going to be offered?"

# CHAPTER TWENTY-NINE

# The Rock

## SEPTEMBER 1830

And so it was that, just a fortnight after my meeting with Commissioner Mayne, I found myself watching Custom House Quay in Falmouth recede as I stood on the deck of the mail packet *HMS Messenger*. The powerful paddle juddered as we set our course, and the water churned and sparkled in the autumn sunshine.

Twelve days later we arrived in Gibraltar. To be honest, when I stepped ashore I vowed never to go to sea again, so rough had been the crossing. Those who have themselves suffered seasickness will know the misery I endured. The heat had steadily increased as we journeyed further and further south; at Cadiz I had reluctantly rejoined the ship after spending a blessedly cool afternoon in the town's cathedral. What delight I took in simple pleasures ashore – birds settling in the trees, and a seat that did not pitch and roll beneath me. And so it was with great relief two days later that I heard a sailor cry out, "The Rock!" and I hurried to join my fellow passengers on deck as we approached Gibraltar.

It was not simply a rock, as I had feared. Certainly the sheer grey walls rearing above us – apparently to a height of well over a thousand feet – were dramatic, but where they levelled off into plateaux there was greenery. Later I would find that these were enclosures known as the Farms; they covered a mere ten acres in total, but were cultivated so carefully and so efficiently that they produced vegetables of all kinds throughout the year. That said, by the end of my stay in the colony, I was thoroughly sick of the local artichoke, which seemed to accompany every meal. The town itself clung to the least sloping area – the skirt of the rock, as I later described it to Martha. A man standing beside me, a regular visitor to Gibraltar, pointed out a green patch that he said was the finest garden in the colony – that belonging to Mount Pleasant, the home of the Naval Commissioner. And after so many long, hot, uncomfortable days at sea, I longed to stroll in its dappled shade.

I was quartered in a neat little room in the police barracks on Castle Street, in the middle of the town, and in deference to my status I was given the room to myself.

On my first full day in Gibraltar, I woke at about seven to the raucous call of gulls wheeling overhead, and pushed open the shutters to look down into the street. A small courtyard was laid out below, with stone benches around the edge and trees to provide shelter. Even in late September, the light was whiter and fiercer than at the height of summer in London, and powerful perfumes drifted from blossoms. I was not due to meet the governor until ten, so I did as a good policeman will always do. I decided to explore my new surroundings and learn what I could about them and their inhabitants.

Leaving the barracks I turned down Castle Steps, and the buildings crowded up on either side of me, keeping the narrow passageway in constant shade. Over my shoulder, the rock loomed. Although some things were familiar, such as the English names on the corners of the streets and over the shops, the inhabitants of the colony were a rare mixture, even to one who has often patrolled the docks of London. An unmistakably English gentle man passed me in a surtout and black neckcloth, only to tip his hat to two elderly Spanish ladies wearing black lace shawls and concealing their faces behind fans. They in turn moved to the side of the street to give way to a mounted British officer in scarlet uniform. Three young women giggled as they watched him, each wearing a red cloak trimmed with black velvet, which I later learned marked them out as women native to Gibraltar, almost certainly descended from Genoese families.

I reached a larger square, and standing in a group were six Moors, all wearing turbans, baggy trousers and wide crimson belts. Sitting cross-legged near them, in the shade of a tree, with bare legs and sandals, black caps and beards, were some Barbary Jews, who work as porters and labourers. In my time in Gibraltar, I learnt to distinguish quickly between these and others, between the sea captains and the sailors with their distinctive rolling walk, and the Andalusian traders with their dark eyes and skin, and even the kilted soldiers, their rough complexion bearing testament to a youth spent exposed to highland wind and rain. Tiny Gibraltar attracted and served them all.

As I had told Martha, Gibraltar had not long since suffered a terrible epidemic of yellow fever, and it was soon clear to me how such a disease could easily take hold. For a start, the houses of Gibraltar were built to a design suited to the latitude of England, yet situated in the latitude of Africa. Not one adaptation to the hot climate had been made: there were no patios, no fountains, no open galleries admitting a free circulation of air, such as I had seen in Cadiz. All was tightly boxed up, as if for the rough climate of London; closed doors, narrow passages and cramped stairways kept out the fresh air and allowed the foul to fester. Having been held on a ship in the harbour for a month thanks to fever ashore when he arrived in 1814, Sir George Don was more than aware of the shortcomings of the colony, and when he was made governor he set about improving sanitation, building a hospital and creating the Alameda Gardens for the people to enjoy fresh air and open space – both in very short supply in Gibraltar. Thanks to these progressive efforts, which suggested a man of conscience and imagination, I was looking forward to meeting the governor, and later that morning I set off for his residence at the Convent, as the fine building was still known even though the friars had moved out a century earlier.

In manner, Sir George reminded me very much of Commissioner Mayne, and I began to see how the two men had found that they were in accord on plans for the new Gibraltar Police. My distant admiration for the governor soon turned into genuine liking and even – I would like to think friendship. When I first saw him, he was standing by his bookcase, scanning the shelves, but as I was shown in he turned to me, hand outstretched in welcome, a wide smile lighting his face. He was shorter than I am, with close-cropped fair hair, and eyes that spotted the fun and mischief in everything.

"Sergeant Plank! The very fellow. Welcome, welcome, welcome. I cannot tell you how delighted I am that you are come to help us. Mayne has only the highest praise for you." He waved me into a chair and handed me a glass of water. "Not to worry – drawn from our own well in the north – perfectly safe. Was your voyage very trying? Not much of a sailor myself – happier on land, with the scent of the earth. After all, God gave me legs and not fins, did he not? Now I daresay you'll be keen to hear what we have in mind for you."

I nodded; it was clear that Sir George was not a man who needed much prompting to talk.

"As soon as I heard about the Metropolitan Police, I knew that I had found the solution. No doubt you've had a walk around the town? So you can see our problem. Gibraltar today has a population of about ten thousand, with just over two thousand being native to the place – the rest, well, you've seen 'em! But on top of that we have the ships coming and going, and the garrison, and keeping it all quiet is daily growing harder. Our local peace officers have been doing their best, but they're outnumbered and, frankly, outclassed. Take a look at this...." He slid a sheaf of papers across the desk to me; across the top I read *Gibraltar – Charter of Justice – the First of September 1830.* "So now we have a Supreme Court, and we need to ensure that we show that we know how to use one. In short, Sergeant Plank, we need a professional police force – and we need it quickly."

For the next six or seven weeks, I worked every hour that God sent, and a few more that I found from somewhere. Sir George was right: the peace officers were well-meaning, but they were a ragtag bunch, with no discipline and only the barest understanding of the law and how to administer it. Each day I concentrated my instruction on a particular aspect of the job, from quelling a disturbance to clearing the narrow streets when they became blocked with carts and horses, from inspecting the brothels to writing up crime reports to pass on to the magistrate. I smartened up the recruits, and tried to instil in them the importance of the dignity of the police officer – that he must be calm and sober, and not do anything to cause people to laugh at him or fear him or mistrust him. Some were unequal to the changes, but the majority worked with a steady determination, and by the time I left I was able to present Sir George with a good body of men, smart in their blue frock coats, with a black armlet to be worn to indicate when they were on duty. As befitted Gibraltar, I made sure to include men who could speak English, Spanish and Llanito – a local dialect seemingly drawn from all the languages of the world. And when I boarded the packet, I was proud to see four of them saluting me from the dock while the rest of the new Gibraltar Police were about their work elsewhere in the town, under the control of Mr Henry Morgan – a very able fellow whom Sir George and I had chosen together.

But I am getting ahead of myself, talking about leaving. With steamers arriving daily to load up with coal, packets calling on their routes to and from England, and traders from all lands congregating in its shady squares and lanes, Gibraltar was always full of gossip, and its people liked nothing better than to add to their store of information. One evening, as I patrolled the streets near the garrison with Constable Carrera – a young officer showing much promise but still liable to distraction – he quizzed me about life as a policeman in London. Like many Gibraltarians, he had dreams one day of seeing the city for himself. And like many young men, his taste for details ran to the grisly.

"Did you see many hangings?" he asked as we slowed to watch the unsteady progress of a couple of soldiers, clinging to each other for support as they returned from squandering their pay in some tavern or other. "Is it true that the body jerks for minutes afterwards?"

"I have seen many people die on the scaffold, yes," I replied. "Although I wish I had not. It is not an entertainment – despite what the size of the watching crowd might suggest."

"What is the biggest crowd you've ever seen?"

"That's easy: Henry Fauntleroy, 1824, one hundred thousand people."

My companion stopped dead, his mouth open in amazement. "A hundred thousand? That's..." he paused to work it out, "that's ten times the entire population of Gibraltar! To watch one man hang. What did he do? Was he a murderer?"

"A forger. I arrested him at his bank; he forged people's signatures on documents so that he could sell their assets without their knowing."

Just then a door was flung open and a man tumbled out into the street on the point of someone else's boot, putting an end to our discussion. But that night, as I lay sweating in bed and thinking wistfully of the cool autumn evenings of home, I found that once again I could not get Henry Fauntleroy out of my mind.

At the end of that week, I was writing my reports on the officers under my training – the governor insisted on regular bulletins on their progress – when Constable Carrera burst into the police office.

"Running again, constable?" I said without looking up from my papers. "Steady and calm, if you please, steady and calm."

"But sir, you must come quickly," he said, dancing from foot to foot. "It is leaving soon, and then he will be gone."

I laid down my pen. "What is leaving, and who will be gone?"

"The packet for Marseille, and the Italian with it – Algenini, no, Angelini."

"Angelini?" It was a name I had not heard for six years, but the mention of it took me back instantly to those cold stone passageways, that reek of desperation, the terrible final crash of that wooden trapdoor.

Carrera nodded. "He said he knows you, and he has something to tell you – but you must hurry, sir – they are to catch the evening tide."

# CHAPTER THIRTY

# The death of hope

TUESDAY 23ᴿᴰ NOVEMBER 1830

Always a slight man, Edmund Angelini was thinner than ever. Were it not for the sun-darkened hue of his skin, he would have looked unhealthy. His fingers plucked nervously at his cuffs as he glanced over his shoulder at the packet, where the crew were making final preparations for the next stage of their journey.

"I could hardly believe it when I overheard the harbour master telling our captain that you were here in Gibraltar," he said as we sat side by side on a low wall in the shade. "There surely cannot be more than one London police officer called Samuel Plank, I thought to myself, and indeed here you are." He seemed distracted.

"Was there something you wanted to see me about in particular, Signor Angelini," I asked, "or is it simply to look at a familiar face far from home?"

"Home?" he asked with a harsh, humourless laugh. "It is a long time since I thought to have a home. You have a wife, sir, and children, no doubt."

"Not children, no."

He looked directly at me for the first time. "A great sadness to you, I am sure."

We sat in silence for a while, watching the porters scampering up and down the ramps like monkeys.

"He has children, you know," Angelini said suddenly, "although he never talks of them. A boy, and two girls. What manner of man can turn his back on his children? At first I hoped he would send for them, and then I hoped he would find a way to let them know of his whereabouts – and then I stopped hoping."

I realised that I was sitting absolutely motionless, as if next to a timid bird that would take flight at the smallest movement. The wrong question would scare him off. Keeping my voice gentle, I asked, "Why did you stop hoping?"

Angelini looked past me into the distance, and I could see tears glittering in his eyes. He spoke quietly. "Because he changed. Or maybe I changed. But he was not the man I had thought he was. He was not noble or betrayed: he was greedy and self-serving. He told me that he needed time away from England to muster his defence and gather evidence for an appeal, but that was never his plan. When I first read about his case, I was filled with outrage and sympathy, and I resolved to do everything I could – I even offered my life in exchange for his. Of course: you will remember that." I nodded. "When I was refused, I asked to be allowed to visit him in his cell to say farewell." He stopped and angrily dashed a tear from his cheek. "That was when he told me what he had worked out, and what he wanted me to do."

I tried not to let my emotion show, but I held onto the wall so tightly that my knuckles turned white. "And what was that?" I asked.

Angelini turned to look at me. "If I tell you, will I be forced to return to England? Will I face the noose? He said that if I ever tell anyone, I am as guilty as he." I shook my head. "My interest is in him, not in you. As far as the authorities in London need know, I heard this from a sailor passing through Gibraltar. Your name will never be mentioned."

He gripped my arm, his bony fingers surprisingly strong. "I have your word?"

"You have my word."

"He had no intention of dying, of course. He said all the right things to the right people – the keeper, that in-

sufferable clergyman – about going to meet God with re-
morse in his heart. But all along he was thinking, planning. Some urged him to flee; he had friends enough who
could have paid the turnkeys to turn a blind eye while he
was spirited out of Newgate – but then..."

"But then," I said slowly as I pieced together the story,
"but then he would have been a hunted man for the rest
of his days."

Angelini nodded. "Always looking over his shoulder,
jumping at every sound – he'd had enough of that, he said.
The only way for him to be truly free was for everyone to
watch him hang. You remember the crowd, Constable
Plank – and every one of them would swear on their
mother's life that they saw him swing from the rope and
die before their eyes."

"As would I...."

"But he knew that the scaffold that they used at Newgate – the new drop, I think they call it – was designed so
that when the door opened, the prisoner fell only eight-
een inches. Not enough to kill you straight off. So that
the crowd could watch you twist and turn for a bit
longer."

I shook my head. "Signor, if you had seen the older
scaffold, the long drop, at work as I have done – sometimes the drop was so great that the head of the hanged
man was jerked clean off. The new drop was meant to be
merciful."

He shrugged. "Well, it certainly was in his case. Wontner, being a decent man, was determined that those hanged on his watch should die as painlessly as possible, and so he regularly stationed two men beneath the scaffold to pull on the prisoner's legs as he dropped, to end it all quickly."

"So you made sure that you were one of these men?"

"There was me, and a turnkey that he had bribed – this man had seen it work before and he was the one who suggested it. So as soon as his feet appeared through the trapdoor, the turnkey and I each took hold of one and held them at a level that made it look to the observers like he was hanging, but really we were supporting his weight. After a suitable interval, he was cut down and we were able to carry him away."

"What about the hangman? Did he not want the clothes?"

Angelini shook his head. "Bribed also. As arranged, we carried the body out of the yard and put it into a coffin in a cart that was waiting. I went back into the prison yard, and made sure that Mr Wontner saw me weeping, as though I was mourning."

"And the body?"

"The next time I saw him was at Falmouth, three days later. I had made my way there on the mail coach; he had private transport. When we boarded the packet I made certain not to acknowledge him, beyond nodding to him in greeting as I did to all of my fellow passengers. He had disguised himself, of course – his likeness was well-known at that time.

"We were twelve in total, so of necessity he and I were often thrown together – but we did not talk of the other matter at all, for fear of being overheard. The voyage was not comfortable – at that time of year, the winds are fierce and the seas attacked us constantly. After about a week we arrived in Cadiz."

"Was that your final destination?"

Angelini nodded. "He did not tell me until we were in sight of the land – perhaps he thought that if I knew in advance I would let something slip – but as the ship turned towards the coast, he told me to gather my belongings as we would be going ashore. After endless days of being thrown around like a child's toy, I was relieved to hear it. The land, which had appeared mountainous, as we drew nearer revealed a gently sloping area with a tidy town and several pretty castles, and I was happy with his choice. You will have seen it yourself on your own voyage." I nodded and he continued. "We made our way into the Bay of Cadiz, and awaited the attentions of the quarantine officers. Once they had given us permission to proceed – although how they, with their unshaven faces and dirty hands, could judge our cleanliness, I was uncertain – we were permitted to go ashore. Four other passengers alighted with us for exercise, but we were the only ones to stay."

The packet lying in the harbour gave a long signal on its whistle and Angelini jumped up. "I must go – I cannot be left behind. I have a strange longing to see Venezia again, after all these years."

I caught hold of his arm. "But Signor Angelini, why did you risk so much for this man?"

The Italian turned to look at me, his eyes as full of misery as any I have ever seen. "Because I loved him. Because I love him. The heart cannot choose where it settles, constable."

I pressed his arm gently, hoping to convey my understanding. "So why leave him now?" I asked. "Why, after six years?"

"Because he lied to me. He told me that it was all a mistake, that people had misunderstood him, and that he intended to return to clear his name. But none of that was true. Here...." He reached into his jacket pocket and handed me a much folded and re-folded piece of paper. "I found this. I left him the same day. I told him that I was taking it as a form of protection – that if he came after me I would hand it over to the police."

"And has he come after you?"

"Not yet. But even if he does not, I cannot carry his secret any longer. When I docked here and heard your name, I knew that it was providence, that I was meant to tell you everything."

"And is he still in Cadiz?" I asked as Angelini turned again towards the sea.

"Almost certainly. He is too ill to go anywhere. Dying, I believe – at last." He dashed a tear from his cheek with the back of his hand. "But there is something else. I was going to keep it – after all, there is little enough that he gave to me – but meeting you means that I can set this one thing right." He pulled a watch from his waistcoat pocket, unclipped it, pressed it to his lips and then handed it to me. It was the one that Wontner had admired all those years ago. "It should go to his son," he said. I nodded. And he was gone, hurrying up the gangplank.

As I looked down at the watch and the paper in my hands, I realised that not once had Angelini mentioned the name of the man from whom he ran. But then he had no need to: for him, no-one else had mattered for the past six years.

# CHAPTER THIRTY-ONE

# They shall smart for it

TUESDAY 23ᴿᴰ NOVEMBER 1830

I walked back towards the town, shielding my eyes from the evening sun slicing between the sheds on the dockside. I passed through a gate in the King's Bastion, following the route that had already become so familiar to me. Only once I was in my own room at the barracks, the door shut tight against visitors, did I take the folded paper from my pocket and read it.

The top half the sheet of paper contained a table of names and figures, starting with "Frances Young, £5,000". At first I thought I was looking at the list of Fauntleroy's forgeries that had been read aloud in court. After the names I still remembered – Elizabeth Fauntleroy, Jedediah Kerie, Lady Nelson – came the confession that had sealed Fauntleroy's fate with the jury. But unlike the one read aloud in court, this list did not end with his signature dated the seventh of May 1816: it continued below it. On and on went the columns of names and amounts, with the last dated only a few days before I had arrested Fauntleroy in his bank. And scrawled in the margin, in a hand marred by ink spots of the kind that are inevitable when you take up your pen in anger, was this: "The Bank began first to refuse our acceptances, and thereby began to destroy our credit. They shall smart for it. HF."

I stared at the paper, reading it again and again. The list found in the tin case in the bank's parlour and used to such devastating effect in court had told only part of the story. And that story was completed at last by the sheet I held in my hand. Henry Fauntleroy had committed forgery not to help his bank survive for the sake of its customers (as he had claimed), nor to feather his own nest (as so many had believed), but simply to take revenge on an institution that had snubbed him. And he had done it for many more years than anyone had realised. The Bank of England had refused to extend his credit, and so he had resolved to embarrass them by exposing the weakness of their controls, eventually dragging their governor into court to hear it all for himself. They shall smart for it indeed.

I let the paper fall onto the desk. At last I had the answer to that question that had so troubled me: why such a man would risk so much. And I knew now what I had to do.

"Well, sergeant, we shall be sorry to see you go – can we not tempt you to stay?" The governor opened his arms wide as if to indicate all that Gibraltar had to offer.

I shook my head. "I have enjoyed working with your men, sir, and I am confident that they will serve you well. But this other matter now needs my attention."

"Indeed. A hanged man turning up alive – you don't see that too often."

"And until I do see it, sir, I will not rest. But if it is true, it is my duty to return this man to England to face the sentence passed by the court."

"It bodes well for my police force, Sergeant Plank, that they have been guided by a man who takes that duty so seriously." Sir George stood and held out his hand. "I wish you every success, and only hope that the voyage to Cadiz is not too rough. I myself would not relish facing the Western Ocean at this time of year."

# CHAPTER THIRTY-TWO

# Plaza de San Antonio

## DECEMBER 1830

And indeed, as the governor warned, it is most unwise to strike out into the Western Ocean in December. By the end of the short voyage I was praying for death. I cursed the Gibraltarian police officer who had advised me to make the journey to Cadiz by sea rather than tackling the mule track in winter; to my mind, sinking up to my knees in mud would have been far preferable.

Our first two hours at sea were deceptively gentle, sheltered as we were in the Strait of Gibraltar; I stood on the deck and watched as we rounded Europa Point, marvelling at the spectacle of the rock above us. We kept close to the Spanish side, particularly as we made our way through the narrowest part of the strait – the Gut, they call it – and took care that our colours were flying. If a captain neglects to do this, the garrison in Gibraltar will fire a blank shot as a reminder, and then real ones if not swiftly obeyed.

Once we emerged into open sea and turned north towards Cadiz, all musings on the beauty of the rock and the activities of the garrison were driven from my mind as we felt the full force of the winter winds. I gazed longingly at the shore, where the town of Tarifa could be glimpsed through the rain, wondering what had possessed me to cast in my lot with a small wooden vessel on a vast and angry sea, until I was driven below deck by the stinging assault of the salt water on my face.

Of the eight passengers on board, just three of us made an appearance at the midday meal – and I will confess that I managed the soup only. All through the afternoon and night the squall blew and the sea was high, and our poor packet groaned and crawled her way up the Spanish coast. I need not elaborate on the discomfort of my own condition. Shortly before dawn, I was relieved to feel the motion abate somewhat, and I fell into a wretched sleep for two or three hours.

At breakfast I forced myself to swallow some plain bread – the captain having recommended it as a way to settle the stomach – and then went on deck for some fresh air. What a difference! The wind had dropped, the sea had calmed, and we were making steady progress. For most of the morning we were out of sight of the land, but just before noon we turned our nose eastwards and headed for Cadiz.

As I stood on deck, loath to go below again where I had been so miserable, I was able gradually to make out what I thought at first were the masts of other ships, but were in fact the distant and numerous spires of churches. They looked very fine, and I was doubly pleased at the prospect of going ashore – both to feel firm ground beneath my feet, and to further explore the town that I had briefly admired on my outward voyage. We finally dropped anchor in the Bay of Cadiz at about five o'clock, and waited for the quarantine officers – but I daresay they did not fancy the twenty minutes' rowing it would take to get to us, and we were forced to spend the night at anchor. At eight o'clock the next morning, they finally boarded, made their inspection, and cleared us to go ashore.

As we made our final approach in a rowing boat, Cadiz revealed more of its white, lofty beauty. We tied up alongside a broad dock, punctuated at the far end by three handsome white marble columns topped with statues. Between us and the town itself was a high wall of hewn stone, surmounted with cannon and in excellent repair.

In the company of two other gentlemen who were disembarking here, I walked through a narrow gateway in the wall, past armed soldiers, and into Cadiz itself. Accustomed as I had become to the narrow alleyways of Gibraltar, I was struck at once by the breadth and brightness of the streets. Substantial dwellings were built on either side, with not a spot to stain their virgin whiteness. There were crowds of people everywhere, the men well-dressed for the most part in voluminous winter cloaks, and the women without bonnets but wearing instead what I now knew was a mantilla – a black lace shawl covering the head and shoulders and cascading to the waist.

My companions were engaged in business at the consul's house and, having no other plan of my own and being curious to see it, I accompanied them. Leading to the house was an elegant avenue, shaded by trees and with a white marble balustrade and seats running along its length. At the end was an archway through which we could see into a courtyard paved with pieces of different coloured marble that glittered in the winter sunshine. Here I took my leave of my fellow travellers, not wishing to intrude upon their business, and turned back towards the town. As I walked away down the avenue, one of the gentlemen came bustling after me.

"I almost forgot to tell you," he said. "The best aspects are from the ramparts – a walk along them at dusk is unmatched." I thanked him for his recommendation, and resolved to do just as he suggested once I had found lodgings.

Cadiz being now a thoroughly mercantile town (as a free port it attracts those who wish to engage in illicit trade with the rest of Spain, principally in tobacco from Havannah and calicos from Manchester) it was not hard to find a room in a tavern, and I was able to leave my bag and set off on further explorations. My companion had been right: the views from the town's ramparts were delightful. I could see the bay itself, the opposite shore and the many towns that sprinkled it, the distant mountain ranges, the vessels lying at anchor in the harbour, the innumerable small boats criss-crossing the bay, and a fine irregular line of handsome white buildings in the park. For a boy from the backstreets of London, it was quite a sight.

But, diverting as it was, I was in Cadiz on a police matter, not an excursion, and the next morning I started making enquiries. No matter the language, the same places are always ripest with information: taverns and brothels. With a few coins to tempt the indiscreet, and no shortage of English customers in both types of establishment willing to act as interpreters, I soon found what

I wanted. It seems that two Englishmen had arrived in Cadiz some five or six years previously, with very little luggage. They had taken rooms at a house in town, and had since lived a quiet life, bothering no-one and receiving few visitors. About a fortnight earlier, the younger man – who had an Italian name that no-one could remember – had disappeared. The older man could be found most evenings sitting in Plaza de San Antonio, watching the people of Cadiz promenading past him in their finery.

That evening, once the sun had set, I walked through the crowded streets to Plaza de San Antonio. Unlike in London, where the city at night belongs to drinkers and revellers and trouble-makers, Cadiz in the evening was alive with families, with groups of ladies walking together unaccompanied, with elderly couples sitting companionably on benches. How my Martha would have enjoyed the opportunity to see what the other ladies were wearing, and to speculate about whether this young couple was engaged to be married, or that elegant gentleman sitting alone was waiting for a friend or his wife or a lover.

For my part, I scanned the face of every man I saw. Six years since I had last seen him: the banker would be well into his middle years, browned by the Spanish sun, perhaps rounded out by years of comfortable living, but now overtaken by illness.

The plaza was formed of a central area, where people gathered in groups to talk, surrounded by trees doubtless intended to afford shade in the summer months, and then encircled by a mosaic-paved area where the general agreement was that one walked. The buildings facing onto the plaza were grand houses peppered with windows and balconies, and many of them had restaurants and cafés on the ground floor, with tables set up outside. I guessed that this is where a man such as Henry Fauntleroy would sit, watching the promenade but not part of it. I resolved to make a slow circumnavigation of the plaza, starting at the soaring twin pink towers of the church.

I had walked around most of the plaza and was returning to my starting point at the church when I caught sight of a man sitting alone at a small table. I could see him only in profile, but it was a profile with which I was extremely familiar. I had stood beside it at three hearings, a trial and an appeal. I had studied it many times from the doorway of a cell. And I had last seen it on a scaffold. The man at the table drained his glass and turned to signal with it to the waiter. He caught me watching him and looked at me for a long moment. Suddenly his eyes widened; the glass in his hand fell to the ground and shattered into a thousand shards.

He made no effort to get to his feet and so I walked over to him. "Henry Fauntleroy?" I asked, although I was certain. But now looking at his face rather than his profile, I was shocked. Far from growing fat on the easy life in Cadiz, his cheeks had fallen in, and his eyes were ringed with dark shadows. As he finally stood to greet me, he had to steady himself on the table, and his hand trembled as it shook mine.

"Constable Plank," he said flatly. "Still a policeman, then, and in Cadiz."

"Sergeant now," I said. "And you? Are you still a banker? There are plenty of opportunities for you here, I daresay."

He shook his head. "I lost the taste for it." We both sat, and when the waiter came over to sweep up the broken glass Fauntleroy ordered two more drinks. "No, I live a very quiet life now. A few friends in England remember me kindly, and make occasional contributions to my living expenses. And Edmund was a good companion, as they go. Until he went. I take it that he is why you are here?"

I nodded. "We met by chance in Gibraltar. He showed me this." I took the folded paper out of my pocket. He looked at it but did not take it from me, and I returned it to my pocket.

"I am afraid, Constable Plank, that there are very few people in life whom you can trust absolutely. Although I am sure that you, as a police officer, know that only too well." He lifted the glass the waiter had placed on the table in front of him and tipped it towards me in salute.

"Surely you could have turned to your family? Your brother, the lawyer – he would have helped."

"Heavens, no! As far as they are concerned, I died on that scaffold."

I stared at him. "Are you saying that you have let them mourn you all these years – your mother, your wife – Maria and your children? That you haven't let them know that you are alive and well?"

"What would be the point of that? They would only insist that I return to England and begin the wretched business of an appeal all over again. I never wanted to plead not guilty and go through the charade of a trial, and appeals, and petitions. It would have been much simpler to go straight from cell to scaffold, as I had planned." He drained his glass. "No: it is better this way. And as you can surely see, constable, I may be alive but I am certainly not well."

I did not trust myself to answer. I remembered his reluctance to follow Harmer's advice, his desperate insistence on pleading guilty – ostensibly because it was the truth and therefore the right thing to do, but in reality so that he could make his escape all the sooner. How could a man could be so cruel, so selfish, as to let those who loved him suffer on his account? I thought back to the pale and shaking John Fauntleroy, determined to do all he could for his brother. I remembered the courtroom tears shed by Maria Finch, and Marianne Fauntleroy's dignified offer to sell her belongings to recoup some money for her husband's customers. And poor Edmund Angelini, who had believed all those years that the plan was to formulate a defence and return to England. Fauntleroy had never had any such intention: I could see that now. I put down the glass that I had been about to raise to my lips; to drink with such a man would have choked me.

I stood. "I am afraid that it is no longer your choice. Henry Fauntleroy, I am an officer of the Metropolitan Police Force of London, who has apprehended you as a fugitive from justice, and as such it is my duty to inform you that we will be returning to London together. I shall enquire as to available berths on the next Falmouth packet, and notify you. Where do you reside?" I pulled out my notebook and jotted down the address he gave me. "I shall call on you after breakfast tomorrow; please make sure to have your personal effects packed and ready."

I briefly considered contacting the local police and asking for a guard to be posted outside the banker's rooms, but I was uncertain how they might react to a foreign police officer arresting a man in their town – and one look at Fauntleroy told me that he was in no condition to escape into the wild countryside inland of Cadiz. As I walked off across the plaza, I glanced back at the banker and saw him take my glass from the table and drain that drink too.

The next morning I made my way to the office of the Falmouth packet company and booked berths on the packet leaving for England two days later. Then, with the young son of the tavern owner scampering alongside me to show me the way, I called on Fauntleroy in his lodgings. He had rooms off a courtyard in a house that must once have been splendid but was now down on its luck. The woman who answered my knock at the front door was dressed in extravagant black, and I guessed that she was a widow trying to survive on what her husband had left her – by the looks of it, a house and plenty of debt. She indicated a stairway to the upper floor and then pointed at a door in the corner which I took to be Fauntleroy's.

When I reached the door, I rapped on it and called my name. The door swung open, as though expecting me, and it was at that moment that I knew. The body on the bed was dressed neatly, the hair brushed as I remembered, a pillow placed against the head to muffle the sound of the pistol.

Propped up on the mantelpiece was a note addressed to me. I unfolded it, expecting, well, I am not sure what I was expecting. A confession? An apology? Neither was in character for Henry Fauntleroy. What he had written, on the other hand, was entirely suited to him.

"Constable Plank," it said. "Please inform the Bank of England that the accounts are now balanced."

## ABOUT THE AUTHOR

Susan Grossey graduated from Cambridge University in 1987 and since then has made her living from crime. She advises financial institutions and others on money laundering – how to spot criminal money, and what to do about it. She has written several non-fiction books on the subject of money laundering, as well as contributing monthly articles to the leading trade magazine and maintaining a popular anti-money laundering blog.

"Fatal Forgery" is her first work of fiction.

CPSIA information can be obtained
at www.ICGtesting.com
Printed in the USA
FSOW01n1301110516
20345FS